Disintegration in Four Parts

**Jean Marc Ah-Sen
Emily Anglin
Devon Code
Lee Henderson**

*with illustrations by
Dakota McFadzean*

Coach House Books, Toronto

Coach House Books acknowledges the financial support of the Government of Canada. We are also grateful for generous assistance for our publishing program from the Canada Council for the Arts and the Ontario Arts Council. Coach House Books also acknowledges the support of the Government of Canada through the Canada Book Fund.

LIBRARY AND ARCHIVES CANADA CATALOGUING IN PUBLICATION

Title: Disintegration in four parts / Jean Marc Ah-Sen, Emily Anglin, Devon Code, Lee Henderson.

Names: Ah-Sen, Jean Marc, 1987- author. | Anglin, Emily, 1979- author. | Code, Devon | Henderson, Lee, 1974- author.

Description: Four novellas.

Identifiers: Canadiana (print) 20210204087 | Canadiana (ebook) 20210204192 | ISBN 9781552454244 (softcover) | ISBN 9781770566620 (EPUB) | ISBN 9781770566637 (PDF)

Subjects: LCSH: Canadian fiction—21st century. | CSH: Canadian fiction (English)—21st century.

Classification: LCC PS8329.1 .D57 2021 | DDC D813/.608—dc23

Disintegration in Four Parts is available as an ebook: ISBN 978 1 77056 662 0 (EPUB); 978 1 77056 663 7 (PDF)

Purchase of the print version of this book entitles you to a free digital copy. To claim your ebook of this title, please email sales@chbooks.com with proof of purchase. (Coach House Books reserves the right to terminate the free digital download offer at any time.)

Table of Contents

'All purity is created through resemblance and disavowal.'

Merz in the Arctic Circle

Lee Henderson

Even as he flees Lysaker, Kurt Schwitters sings:

Kwiiee kwiiee
kwiiee kwiiee
kwiiee kwiiee
kwiiee kwiiee
kwiiee kwiiee
kwiiee kwiiee

What is the matter with you, Schwitters?

He's heard this question before, many times. Ever since childhood. What's the matter with you? What's the matter with you, Schwitters?

Something *must* be the matter with Kurt Schwitters.

In Berlin they said, What is the matter, Schwitters? Are you a degenerate? Are you insane? Berlin, cultural capital of the known universe. He's got a silver tooth in his jaw as keepsake from that night twenty years ago when a purebred Berliner in the audience at a cabaret coldcocked him midway through a performance of the *Ursonate*. The inventor of Merz, forever misunderstood.

Alas, Schwitters can't escape the critics. He and his son might have both fled Germany but the epithets followed. Even his dear son Ernst, his own son of all people, will dabble in it. What is the matter with you, Schwitters? Ernst says. In Norway, he signs his photographs *Ernst Guldahl*, disguising his affiliation with Merz by the use of wife's surname.

What's the matter with you?
What is your emergency, Schwitters?
Are you damaged?
Are you drunk?
Are you deranged?

Yes.
I am Merz.
Everything is the matter with Merz.
Merz is the world.
Merz is Merz.

Rakete rinnzekete
rakete rinnzekete
rakete rinnzekete
rakete rinnzekete
rakete rinnzekete
rakete rinnzekete

The Kabelvåg post office receives an urgent cable before dawn. The noise awakens the clerk, who lives in the attic. The Nazis have bombed Oslo. Orders to follow. Early spring on the inside edge of one of the southern ports on the Lofoten Islands. People have lived here for thousands of years, and fisherman have fished these seas since long before the Vikings, but most of the surrounding mountains and valleys remain to be explored. Mankind has hardly touched Kabelvåg, and there is a serenity and a peace found in these lands. Kabelvåg barely knows it is part of creation. These pristine mountains still hold their secrets. The ocean teems with schools of skrei, the skies are full of cormorant and puffin, and the near silence in the sheltered bay of Kabelvåg echoes with ancient murmurs from the very beginning of time. Now that immeasurably small sound, which residents of Kabelvåg might privately think of as God, something about Kabelvåg more precious than all their belongings, that pure sound which they felt more than they heard, is bare and exposed. Kabelvåg is unprotected against the roar of German bombers clashing out at sea with British warships. Attacks and counterattacks shake them inside their bomb shelters. And when the fight moves elsewhere there's the sounds of the town carpenters and steelworkers.

In the coming days, they learn their first command is to prepare lodgings for the internment of illegal aliens. German citizens are among the refugees from Oslo and Southern Norway being sent their way. As the first signs of war arrive on their beaches, a well-appointed, newly decorated military man, until recently a local folk arts scholar, waits to greet the fleeing refugees aboard a cod-fishing boat presently docking. From the shining calfskin boots, wool slacks, the dark blue wool overcoat, the fresh lily in the breast pocket, purple pins in his tie knot, and barbered face and neck, Captain Trygve Wicklund looks every bit like it's his first day in uniform.

Welcome to Kabelvåg, he tells the first man to appear out of the hull. I am Headmaster … but I should say you shall know me as *Captain* Trygve Wicklund. Please, watch your step and please queue up over there so that I might –

His first refugee leaps onto the dock and embraces the captain. Loses his balance, tips over, Wicklund helps him regain his footing. I'm not used to a steady floor, says Schwitters. He is a tall man, heavyset, like a plinth, with all his weight on his heels. His eyes are bright and glassy blue like the eyes in a doll. His grin is disconcerting Captain Wicklund. Schwitters takes a deep, glorious inhale until his lungs are busting, as if he'd held his breath the entire voyage at sea.

I am Schwitters. Kurt Schwitters. German citizen, but enemy of the Nazis. Artist of the avant-garde. Cultural refugee. Greetings, my friend, from the landless dispossessed. Here we are, I don't know where, but at the very edge of exile. Let us bless the skipper and his sturdy cod bucket for bringing us out of the hairy soup alive.

Our camp has beds for a hundred and twelve. How many are you? All German?

An incredible assortment of forty-two souls, Schwitters tells him. Painter, poet, inventor, collagist, sculptor, carpenter, carver, portraitist, belletrist, dancer, singer, actor, and now that I've introduced myself let me tell you a little about some of the others on board …

Forty-two, the captain says. He is astonished. Such a small boat. He looks beyond Schwitters and mutters something about how he would like to make an announcement once everyone's disembarked.

Schwitters says, Of course you would, and thank you. Ah! Here come the photographer and dancer, Ernst and Esther Guldahl, my … son and daughter-in-law. Lovely couple. She's from Oslo. He took her name when they got married. Quite natural. In art circles, the Schwitters name is synonymous with *Merz*. Ernst … this is the captain … Captain ah … I already forget.

Wicklund. Captain Wicklund. Now please, move aside. Queue up here.

Ernst, shaking, shivering, mouth hanging open and tongue threatening to fall out of it, he reaches out with one bone-rattling hand and takes the captain by the wrist, leans in to tell him in all confidence and with an eye-watering case of halitosis, *I'm really more her husband than I am his son.*

Ernst hasn't held down much more than a saltine since they fled from Lysaker a month ago, seasick, and no appetite for dodging naval battles and hiding under fog from Nazi warplanes. Deadly draining stuff. And slow. They might as well have walked most of the way. A man's constitution is truly tested at sea during wartimes. It turned Ernst Guldahl into a motion-sick stick of a man who can barely hold himself upright under the weight of a worn-out pinstripe suit and second-hand black sable overcoat. Clothes that fit him a month ago now look boxy and clownish. In peacetime, he might pass for an American matinee idol in the role of star reporter, with a camera slung around his chest on a leather strap like a jungle knife over a crisp white shirt, his sleek black hair tossed up and back in seductive waves. But with his hair hanging down in oily strands over his chalky face, mouth breathing, eyes bloodshot from exhaustion, hobo beard, Ernst looks more like his dad's degenerate German art than a pedigreed calendar photographer. The captain lifts him off the fishing boat and onto the dock like a corpse or a fisherman's mystery catch.

Esther Guldahl's a sprinkle over a hundred and fifty centimetres tall; her hairbun can't tickle her husband's chin if she stands in front of him. But despite her petite stature and the wicked boat ride, she's walking fine, in fact, with a dancer's hop, perfect balance, head held high, ears pricked, eyes afire, and complexion hale, and still strong enough to support her husband's weight when his knees give out. She was raised in the avant-garde and wanted to marry within the avant-garde, so she found a man fleeing the avant-garde.

The view is of snowy mountainous islands and the placid waters between them.

What an eerie afternoon, Schwitters says with a shiver.

Wicklund pulls a gold-plated timepiece out of his breast pocket and checks it. It's three thirteen in the morning, he asserts as if in agreement with Schwitters.

Did you hear that, Esther? It's three in the morning.

In his best German, Wicklund addresses the entire crowd: Now, may I have your attention, please. You are hereby classified by wartime law as enemy aliens until your status as refugee or enemy is determined, and as we process your refugee status you will be interned here and will be under my command. Please follow my senior guardsman Henk and make your way in an orderly row two by two up the road to that schoolhouse you see past the forest.

There had been storms and squalls. The boat got tossed, waves punched it to and fro, waves and rain drenched it. Below deck, the refugees were alternately sick and tired and scared. The deafening noise of the boat bending under the power of the sea, the machine-gun rain, the whistling and howling wind, the enormous chaos of the open ocean, that is all gone now, it is over. This road ahead of Schwitters through this small forest is so safe and beautiful and simple, the path is dappled with shade, the stones are covered in leaves. And they are surrounded by the deep, deep silence of Kabelvåg.

What a serene, painterly silence, says Schwitters. What an amazing silence. It's so quiet, I can even hear the sound of my eyes blinking.

Schwitters is up at the front of the line, marching beside Henk. He's a good head-and-shoulders taller than the guardsman, and as much as he would like to bask in the landscape, he can sense the young man's anxiety from the way he grips that hunting rifle. In a jovial tone, and his best Norwegian, Schwitters says: Give a man a sword or a gun and all of a sudden he feels like he's cast in an opera. Which one are you in? Something with pirates, perhaps?

Excuse me, do you think I won't use it? says Henk.

We had a crate of champagne aboard that we promised to drink once we got ashore, or to bargain with if we had to, Schwitters tells Henk. But after watching the Brits bomb a Nazi warboat chasing us down, we couldn't wait and celebrated early. I made vegetable stew and we drank all the champagne. It was quite the party.

Schwitters reaches into his jacket pocket and Henk jerks on the rifle. Cigars, Schwitters reassures him. Only cigars. We can't toast our safety with the bubbly, but, if you'd like one … you see, they're quite undamaged.

Schwitters has many pockets. His jacket, his blazer, his vest, and his pants all have pockets. Henk is not impressed. Finally Schwitters finds what he's been looking for: his matches. He strikes one and puts the flame to the end of Henk's cigar until it's red and then lights a second match to his own cigar.

What a lovely day, Schwitters says as he puffs.

It's the middle of the night, Henk reminds him.

So I hear. That must be why it's so quiet, he says. The birds are all asleep. What's the population of your town?

There's Jews with you? Henk asks quite abruptly without answering Schwitters.

I never thought to ask, he tells Henk.

You'll all be interrogated.

Yes, but for now, my new friend, I get to take in the sheer splendour of our surroundings. What a beautiful quiet.

I don't believe there's a more beautiful place on earth, says Henk.

Schwitters inhales the sublime quietude. Conifers make a fine canopy of shade over the road, and the ground on either side is covered in a thin green blanket of rock grass sprinkled with a rainbow of wildflowers. The air is so fresh it makes Schwitters's head spin. Henk's thoughts are lost in the grandeur of his new role as guard, Schwitters can tell. But Schwitters is lost in the enormity of this little place, its pathetic grandeur, its ancient isolation.

You are all Germans? says Henk.

I am.

But you speak Norwegian?

I've lived in Lysaker for two years with my son and his wife. And when he was younger, we came often on vacation as a family and so I could paint. I quite love to paint Norway.

And you're a Jew?

No.

We thought there would be Jews.

As I said, I didn't inquire.

But you *are* German?

I am, Schwitters says. And I hope to remain a German citizen my whole life, and to remain *not* a Nazi for even longer.

If there are any among you ... you'll help me root them out?

Schwitters does a second quick study of the young man. Every face is like a leaf, he thinks. Delicate.

You have my word, Henk, Schwitters tells him. And they shake on it.

Kwiiee kwiiee
kwiiee kwiiee
Rakete rinnzekete
rakete rinnzekete
rakete rinnzekete
rakete rinnzekete
rakete rinnzekete
rakete rinnzekete

Everyone and everything is reconditioned for war. War takes a town and makes it a barracks. The local school is repurposed as an enemy alien internment camp. That is what he is now. An enemy alien. He can't go home. He's at their mercy. Schwitters and the other enemy aliens are marched to Kabelvåg's local Vågan Folkehøgskole, for teenagers. A school for the traditional arts and crafts of the region. A centre for creativity and study, with all the tools and materials required, tucked away in Norway's great expanse of nowheredom. Schwitters takes one look at this island on the big map pinned up at the entrance to the school's dorms and shuddered. Truly this was the littlest piece of absolute unheard-of obscurity he could ever imagine. A tiny outpost on the small tailbone of an island at the bottom of what must be dozens of islands and peninsulas stretching like vertebrae on a spine going up Norway's northwestern coast.

Certainly no one in these remote parts can be expected to have ever heard of Merz! And yet what are the chances he find himself interned at an arts and crafts school? He could have ended up at a chicken farm or coal mill. But here he is. Once they are checked in, Wicklund allows the refugees some limited freedom on the surrounding grounds. He's not concerned that anyone will flee. What Schwitters senses is that Wicklund can appreciate that they are refugees, and not of any danger. No one is armed. There's nowhere to go. And Henk promises them he will shoot anyone who tries.

And so Schwitters goes outside with his sketchbook and studies the view. Within sightline he can see three guards at about equidistance and so he knows the camp's boundaries are shallow, but at the same time there is some trust – no perimeter walls. In the very distance beyond the trees he sees little cabins with chimneys smoking, each cabin on a small piece of land with a field of grain, and a fence surrounding pigs, sheep, fowl, a horse, and a low barn. Cows graze certain pastures and not others. The smell is faint in the air.

He settles down on a grassy slope to draw the landscape leading down to the water where they docked and that's how, an hour later, Wicklund finds him. Immediately he is impressed by the speed of Schwitters's hand. Yes, he's drawing to calm his nerves. Trees calm me, Schwitters tells him. Wicklund says that after registering all the refugees he is delighted to learn there are so many artists among those interned. He's been headmaster of this school for the past two decades, and every year he's loved it more and more. Why? Schwitters asks. Wicklund only has to make note of the air, the inspiring solitude, that divine silence, and of course the natural inspiration; for he's not just headmaster, he's an artist, too, Wicklund tells Schwitters. Pointing to Schwitters's sketch as evidence of Kabelvåg's pull on the creative soul. Whether it is the landscape or the air, or its location on earth, Wicklund is certain Kabelvåg's got a special gravity. Maybe it's why his alumni are so renowned. Had Schwitters ever heard of the Folkehøgskole before now? Well it doesn't matter, says Wicklund. This is the first time in the fifty-year history of the school that classes have been suspended. Such a shame. First his students get drafted and now his school gets drafted, too. No desks or chairs anymore, but lots of beds. At least they are for refugees, says Wicklund, and not POWs. Schwitters emphatically agrees. And look at this, Wicklund says and pats the lapels of his jacket, Wicklund's no longer headmaster, he's Captain Wicklund. Still can't get over it.

Schwitters thinks to himself how delighted he is that he's here. Of all places.

We've been around and around and around for days, on and off boats, off and on, on and off, Schwitters tells him. Last week, or the week before, we set out from bombed-out Harstad in a hurry, and before that, it was a narrow escape from Tromsø after fleeing bombed-out Molde, that all started a month ago on the last train out of bombed-out Lysaker. I dearly hope your beloved town isn't next. The light here is so full of grace. Everything is peaceful. You'd think there was no great abyss ripping through the world. Where did you say we are, Commander?

Captain. It's Captain. You're in Kabelvåg. Yes, the Arctic sun is … You're in Kabelvåg, says Wicklund. And the abyss *has* touched us. Everyone in Kabelvåg is on alert. Every day, every night, we think of it, hear of it, fear it.

And I should like to paint this view of Kabelvåg at least once before we set out *again*, says Schwitters and he takes another deep breath. What sort of art supplies do you have on hand, Captain?

If there's an opportunity I would be pleased to provide a personal introduction to our pottery and painting studios, photo darkrooms, and if I can I'll give you a tutorial on the use of our electric circular saw in our woodworking shop, the first of its kind in all of Norway. Cuts a hundred thousand times faster than a man.

An electric circular saw! My goodness, says Schwitters. I should very much like to see it.

Very good, says Wicklund with a laugh. Then we'll be in touch. I see Henk would like to speak to me. Oh, I see it's time for your lunch. It's midday. Good afternoon, Schwittress.

Schwitters.

Wicklund. Oh, I mean –

Good day, Wicklund.

Schwitters.

The dining hall is in a gymnasium set up with twenty tables on the hardwood floors. The kitchen serves hot plates of stew over white bread. It's a step above the vegetable stew Schwitters made and for that Schwitters is pleased. And there's hot tea and coffee. Dessert would be the steamed beets with mint.

Schwitters pushes an imaginary napkin down the front of his shirt collar. What good fortune, says Schwitters with tears in his eyes. My compliments to our chef. For the past six days the only recipe we've tasted is the one for *disaster*.

Welcome to the slow stew of relative peace, says the chef.

It's good to lay eyes on someone who wants us all fed instead of wants us all dead, says Schwitters.

Takes a lot of guts to make a joke, says the man, laughing as he stirs the simmering pot. The smell is intoxicating.

Schwitters pats his belly. Hollow as a drum, he says. Just like my courage. Now fill me up on what's good.

More salt? Let me know. This was a big dinner for me, says the man, who covers his grin and tells Schwitters he is normally the science teacher here at the Vågan Folkehøgskole, but he loves to experiment with recipes, emulsions, explosives, or *food*. Tonight's speciality is the local *tørrfisk* in stew.

Ernst, staring at the yellow coagulate and things protruding from the chef's pot, loses his focus, then his footing, and almost passes out.

Don't hold back, kind fellow, says Schwitters. Chef's special, please. More and more *tørrfisk* stew for me and my son here. We've been through an ordeal.

Very good, sir. *Tørrfisk* for you all.

Just slather me in it, chef, says Schwitters. I'm hungry enough to eat straight from the cooking pot.

He's got the chef laughing now. I'm hardly a chef but here you go.

The man named Köln rears up behind Esther in the queue for supper and in front of twenty others, without a word, budges past her, shoulders his way up to Schwitters, and bumps him out of the way, then drops his hands on the counter so the chef will serve him next. No one argues with Köln.

Köln nods at the chef but says nothing.

Tørrfisk stew, says the chef sharply. He watches Köln watch him stir.

Köln points his nose at simmering pot. He's given his stew first while the others wait.

Would you like to join us at a table, Köln? says Schwitters.

No answer.

Esther helps her husband carry his bowl to a table. Ernst droops along beside, holding on to her shoulder for balance. He's a shell, quite hollow, with a grey-green complexion, and his rank unwashed suit hanging off him like rags. The degenerate artist's son is still so seasick.

What's the matter with you, Schwitters? says Ernst. Can't you see he wants to be left alone?

Ernst's skin burns with fever. He's almost blind. His legs dangle under his hips. His feeble arms. His back aches. His head spins. Schwitters or Esther must support him wherever he goes. He looks at his plate. Fish stew. The aroma puzzles him, the hunger it stimulates. First, a glass of water. Then coffee. Then over the next half hour, Ernst musters enough strength to force the *tørrfisk* down his throat. The first solid food in days.

Once Köln is done his meal he takes his plate back to the kitchen, nods to the science teacher chef as if thanking him for the meal, then without looking back, leaves the gymnasium.

He is the most dangerous man among us, says the artist Müller-Blensdorf, leaning over to speak from his table with Schulz, the philosophy professor. We must stay vigilant.

Well, I know it's the middle of the night but I'm going to my cot to have a nap, says Schulz.

On scrap paper, Schwitters writes:
More salt on the tørrfisk
or leave the man alone?
Stay vigilant or
take a nap?

Three or four hours later, who knows, it might even be twelve hours later the way time stands on its nose here, but Schwitters is still awake. He sketches while the other refugees sleep. His stomach and his mind are full. Bright night, dark visions. Like mud and clay, bitumen, mercury, glue. Faces. Angels. Structures. Secrets. Even here in this silent Nordic limbo, he hears music. In his mind he hears sound sonnets, noise music, gibberish songs. And words, like bits of ash after a fire, float across his inner senses. He's not able to rest like the others. He's profoundly awake.

When his daughter-in-law wakes up (Ernst grinds his teeth in his sleep), she and Schwitters go for a walk together with two other companions, the sculptor Müller-Blensdorf and the academic philosopher, Schulz. Schulz is afraid that at any moment they will hear German bombers, and the fear is so intense in him that it's asphyxiated the blood in his outer extremities, he says, and so not only is he afraid, he's always cold. In fact, says Schulz, the ends of his fingers are numb. He can't feel them. His fingertips are white. He can't get warm. Even when he's dry Schulz feels wet. And he can't stop shivering.

On the grass outside the dorm room, overlooking the bay where they docked, the refugees are looking at the ground for pencils, at Schwitters's request. He can always use another pencil. Müller-Blensdorf can't understand why Schwitters thinks they'll find any pencils out here, but so far Schwitters has found five of various lengths and colours. The others have not found any. Schwitters sketches as they walk. Up above in the blue sky the moon is like a cucumber slice with a bite out of it. The sun is there too, over to the north, minding its own burning business, like a peach so perfect no one dares touch it. The earth is an eggplant. Purple trees, purple grass. Schwitters hasn't found a green pencil crayon yet.

A very fine sketch, he says to himself.

They watch as the sun goes bit by bit behind a violet mountain across the inlet on Austvågøya Island. As if to distract them during the costume change, the sky above them darkens then a part of it opens up to a vast view of the universe.

Schwitters gives a last good suck on his toothbrush, then pops it out of his mouth, and slips it back into a breast pocket of his vest under his sweater under his jacket, all to the complete bafflement of Müller-Blensdorf, who hasn't brushed his teeth in weeks. Schwitters spits and says, Ah, would you look at that … a teeny tiny nighttime.

While the sun is gone they can gaze up at the darkness of space and all the brightest stars. And then they're gone again as Freyja rises up from the horizon and reconquers the sky.

What a strange treat that was, says Schwitters. Not at all like a normal sunset or sunrise.

Quite a vision, says Müller-Blensdorf. Felt like a dream scene in a movie.

That makes Esther wonder aloud if there might be a film projector at the school and perhaps movies they could watch.

Or *make*, says Schwitters. If they have the equipment.

Müller-Blensdorf is dumbfounded. I swear I'll never get over you, Schwitters. I'll never get used to your whims, and it will never cease to shock me what surplus of energy there is in your bean. Will you ever rest, Schwitters? What's the matter with you? he says. My god, man. I just slept for three terrible hours. My head is so foggy and throbbing I can hardly remember my own name. We're prisoners! And you dream of making movies.

Nice if they had some American films, says Schulz wistfully.

Night After Night ... or *The Thin Man*, says Esther. I love those capers.

Give me Mickey Mouse, says Müller-Blensdorf. Something to soothe my children.

Look, there's Köln sitting at that open window up there. He's awake, too, says Schwitters as he waves. Then he shouts, Hello, Köln! Hello! Hi!

Oh my god, leave the man alone, Schwitters, says Müller-Blensdorf.

But instead, Schwitters goes up to the side of the dormitory building where they're interned, below the window, and says to Köln: We're looking for pencils ... but we thought we might instead look for a film projector and some movie reels. Would you like to help us? Who do you prefer, Mae West or Myrna Loy?

Köln does not answer him or look down.

If you can't sleep, at least take your mind off things. I was drawing the countryside. If you'd like a look at my sketches I can bring them up to you.

What is the matter with you, Schwitters? Why must you bother me? Leave me alone.

The first words out of Köln's mouth, the only thing anyone's heard him say since they first met him onboard the cod fisherman's boat. With that, of all the things to hear, Schwitters returns to his friends in the garden, thunderstruck.

Absolutely shaken. Of all the bombs, this one knocked him off his feet. Two camp guards watch Schwitters pass. Schwitters must have been walking like a goose because the local guardsmen with their hunting rifles nod their heads and tighten their grips as he trips past them. The guards are dressed in their hunting gear but there are military badges pinned to their epaulets.

God morgen. Got morgen. Guten morgen, says Schwitters and bows his head. But he passed the guards more than twenty steps ago.

Ppppp-ppppp, Schwitters sings to himself as he lumbers on.
Rakete rinnzekete

rakete rinnzekete

rakete rinnzekete

rakete rinnzekete

rakete rinnzekete

rakete rinnzekete

Beeeee

Sketchbook under his arm, always.

In Schwitters's hand inside his pocket there is a long white soapstone the size of a yam and white as bone. He found it in a field outside Lysaker the day before the invasion, and ever since he fled there a month ago he's been carving it on and off into a Merz. When stripped of any proper tools he sands it with his bare hands and carves it with his fingernails. Thumbnail sanding a groove, he sings:

bö

fö

     böwö

fümmsbö

böwörö
fümmsböwö

Esther finishes a cigarette and stamps it out under the heel of
her shoe. As they all begin to walk back to the school, she says
to Schwitters, What did I tell you? You're not as likable as you
think you are.

You shouldn't ask for trouble, says Müller-Blensdorf. You
make a nuisance of yourself, Schwitters. You're going to get us
all killed.

All our days at sea we whispered about Köln, Schwitters
tells them, no one ever respected his privacy then, we talked
about him at every turn. At least I try to talk *to* him and not
just *about* him.

Leave the man at peace. That's obviously what he wants,
cries Müller-Blensdorf.

Not now. Are you a fool, Müller-Blensdorf? Of all the times
to give up. Why, I *finally* broke his silence. He *just* spoke to me.
You saw for yourselves. He's *cracking.* He didn't crack on the boat.
But I'm cracking him *now.* Some spy. He can't even handle Merz.

He's a Nazi. Don't deny it. Right now, outnumbered,
unarmed, silence is his weapon.

He *just* spoke to me. His weapon is breaking, says Schwitters.
Now who is the fool?

Esther says, Köln is never going to be your friend, Dad.
Whatever he is, Nazi or a refugee like the rest of us, he's not
interested in you, me, or any of us. He's never going to love
Merz or sing your nonsense songs.

That's right, says Müller-Blensdorf. Listen to the wisdom
of your daughter-in-law. Give up, Schwitters. There's no soul

left in the Nazi. He's more likely to murder us before you convert him.

That's when Schulz speaks: As I said many times while we were at sea, and so it remains, that for the moment, all Köln has done is ignore us with his silence. Let's not behave like our enemies, seduced by our worst suspicions.

My thoughts exactly, says Schwitters.

Give the man his privacy if it's what he wants, says Müller-Blensdorf.

Esther kisses her father-in-law on the forehead. Good night, Schwitters, good night, dear Father.

I believe it's the morning.

No, it's midnight.

Midnight? Sleep well then.

For the first time since the beginning of April, Schwitters has a room all to himself. A little dorm with a cot. There's a window. He should be happy. It's as if he's a student again. He can almost pretend it's so. Then he thinks of Helma, his wife. No. Put those memories aside. His parents. No, those, too. He thinks of Höch. Yes, dear Hannah, where are you now? How he misses his old friends. His heart beats with a ferocious will of its own. He throws off his overcoat, searches pockets, pockets upon pockets, until a notebook is found, and goes straight to the most recent page: *Can you hear the machine guns? Don't forget to pack a toothbrush!* He was on the last train out of Lysaker when he wrote that. April 9, '40. He adds today's date, May 3, his location, and after his poem about the salted fish stew he adds the line: *It's tranquil here. Try not to get too comfortable.* When he lies down on the cot he discovers there's a part of him still rolling around out at sea. And if he closes his eyes, the whole world tosses upside down and it feels as though he's being thrown across the school running to look for his son.

> Kwiiee kwiiee
> kwiiee kwiiee!
> Kwiiee kwiiee
> kwiiee kwiiee!
> Rakete rinnzekete!
> Rakete rinnzekete!

The longest stretch below deck was eighteen days, from Molde to Harstad. A perilous, nauseating journey. In Harstad, they were met by the British army, who separated the Germans from the other refugees, and threw them in line for the internment camps. The British navy secured the docks from German bombers while every boat in the area was called in to collect passengers. Escape from Harstad to Kabelvåg was another eight slow days through narrow channels among the Lofoten Islands. Staying near the shore and trying to remain out of sight of German submarines patrolling the Nordic Sea. Shells detonate close enough to feel them rattle the hull, artillery near and far popping and whistling, large explosions and small crackles like fireworks, inhaling diesel fumes from the ship's engine, seasick, vomiting, unable to hold down a solid meal, everyone sick, the widower Müller-Blensdorf's children sobbing in German, *I want to go home, Papa, I want to go home*, wailing, everyone weeping, life seemingly near its end, everyone inconsolable, all except for Schwitters. And Köln. Even Köln has to take care of the Hallbauers' newborn baby from time to time, while both parents heave with seasickness. Other times Schwitters sits down with the seasick sculptor Müller-Blensdorf for an earnest one-way conversation – Müller-Blensdorf says nothing, he's incapacitated with seasickness – about the days of the Weimar, remember the Weimar, Schwitters waxes nostalgic as Müller-Blensdorf retches into a galvanized bucket. Schwitters writes in his diary: *Müller-Blensdorf sick again. Threw up all last night. Asks me, will we see the outside of this whale ever again? Ernst, too, sick.* Until the Nazis levelled it, Schwitters had a studio in a converted church in Oslo. Now his life fits in two suitcases and his only proof of identity is a few newspaper clippings.

When Köln is on the toilet, Müller-Blensdorf motions for Schwitters to come close for a moment. Watch what you say to a Nazi, he whispers.

Schulz, in the cot above, leans down and says, We don't know what he is, remember? But you, Schwitters, we trust you.

Why is that? Schwitters asks.

Müller-Blensdorf says, You have the most outrageous alias if you're a spy. The deepest cover imaginable. A member of the old avant-garde? Loathed by the Nazis and all but ignored by the current art scene. Impressive.

With trust like that, says Schwitters, I'd almost rather have your suspicions.

The ship rolls under them.

Ernst grows worse the longer they're at sea. His legs are jelly. His stomach is in knots and turns over every minute. Everything he puts down comes up right away. Dry heaves consume him day and night. A migraine threatens to smash his skull into pieces from the inside out. He's beyond dizzy. He can't sleep. He writhes in his cot grinding his teeth, forced to listen to his father's mad songs. After all this torment, he's down three stone and skeletal. Esther's moaning and groaning in the cot above Ernst. She sends down a bucket for Schwitters to rinse out. He and Köln collect buckets. Schwitters sings them the *Ursonate* and distracts them with ridiculous fairy tales. Nurse Köln never speaks. Schwitters sings and babbles all day and all night, you can't shut him up, but not Köln. The most they get from Köln is a nod. The moment his back his is turned, their eyes talk. His total silence flusters them. Schwitters just annoys them. Schwitters, that man is an indefatigable absurdity. But among the refugees, Köln is a concern.

Let's go ask the captain when he thinks we'll find safe harbour, says Schwitters to his co-nurse at the washing station. Maybe he's heard something over the wire. What do you think? Let's go.

No answer.

You're right. He'd tell us if he had good news.

The fisherman's wife never knows what her husband wants for dinner, Schwitters tells Köln on another day as they share the sinks, doing everyone's buckets as usual.

No reply. Tricky one. Barracks humour doesn't crack him either, Schwitters thinks to himself.

What if we went up to the captain's quarters and asked him ourselves? What do you say? Let's go.

Completely mute.

Kwiiee kwiiee kwiiee kwiiee! Kwiiee kwiiee kwiiee kwiiee! Rakete rinnzekete! Rakete rinnzekete!

Köln remains stubbornly mute.

They remain aboard far longer than anyone wished for or anticipated, and in their time together misery compounds misery, and most of them are half-dead. Some days they are in a port, escorted by Norwegian or British forces to a nearby way station, like a floating prison, quite like fish in a bucket, but without any way of knowing for how long. Nowhere remains safe long enough for them to disembark. So the illegal aliens are herded further and further north. Schwitters calms himself with sketches, portraits, imaginary landscapes. He conducts one-sided conversations with other refugees. He sings old songs and makes up new ones. He even puts on solo theatricals. While everyone is paralyzed with fear and motion-sick, Schwitters sings. He tells a story about the travails of a two-dimensional man. The tale of a talking scarecrow. One of his parables is called *Normal Insanity*. He bellows and mimes his way through his stories as if he's back onstage at another smoky underground Berlin cabaret. Don't torture your captive audience, hisses Müller-Blensdorf. Schwitters spits nonsense to make the kids laugh. He reminisces with the other artists and writers about gallery debts and cancelled exhibitions, publishers gone bankrupt and exiled. He entertains the children for hours and hours, spitting, cooing, stuttering, and then, when they start singing along, all of a sudden the other refugees realize the mad gibberish isn't so mad after all, and in fact he's repeating the same sounds over and over, hour after hour. *The Ursonate.*

Fümms bö wö tää zää Uu,
                    pögiff,
                              kwii Ee.

Fümms bö wö tää zää Uu,
                    pögiff,

kwii Ee.
Ooooooooooooooooooooooooo

Now the kids all know the *Ursonate*. For them it's like a ridiculous prayer. It keeps their spirits up, an amusement, a distraction.
And then the others catch the bug and can't help themselves –
the grownups learn the *Ursonate*! And soon the *Ursonate*
becomes part of every refugee's daily ritual. A bug in the brain.
A secret code. As the weeks pass, a liturgy forms. They split up
the *Ursonate* into parts. One part in the morning, with an inter-
mission for breakfast. They finish the second part after lunch.
The children start another round before dinner, which the
adults gradually join in. After the children are put to sleep, there
is one round of the adults whispering the entire thing.

Kwiiee kwiiee
kwiiee kwiiee!
Kwiiee kwiiee kwiiee kwiiee!
Rakete rinnzekete!
Rakete rinnzekete!

They sing, cry, vomit, and lament. They sing it in call and
response louder and louder until one side makes a fatal mistake.
They sing the *Ursonate* as a lullaby to the kids and as a love
song to each other. They sing it in their sleep. They sing the
Ursonate as a plea: *Let us find safe harbour.* As a prayer: *End this
madness.* As truth: *We are just silly peaceful people caught up in
this horror.* One by one the choir of the *Ursonate* fades to a
single voice. Schwitters is the last to notice. He turns around:
his son, Ernst – he's stood up! Upright! On his feet, behind
Schwitters this whole time. Ernst! For a moment Ernst says
nothing. In fact, they expect he's going to tell the whole lot of

them to shut up. When he does speak, though, it's not to bark and complain or gag and vomit, he's got the next stanzas of the *Ursonate*. He joins right in. Rakete rinnzekete rakete rinnzekete rakete rinnzekete, says Ernst, and there's cheers and laughter and tears as Schwitters and his son, and his son's wife, all embrace, then everyone below deck joins in.

böwö fümmsbö böwörö
fümmsböwö böwörötää
fümmsböwötää böwörötääzää
fümmsböwötääzää

The Ursonate, a time-consuming, wordless, ridiculous sea shanty. Its nonsense carries them over many waves. Even the boat sings the *Ursonate*. The squeals and creaks of the ship's metal hull. The boat booms when Schwitters booms, whispers when Schwitters whispers. Even the vessel. Even Ernst. Even Ernst.

But Köln does not join in. Köln will not join in. He won't sing along.

rakete rinnzekete
rakete rinnzekete
rakete rinnzekete
rakete rinnzekete
rakete rinnzekete
rakete rinnzekete

Schwitters wakes hearing screams. He's back in the craft school, the internment camp. He's in Kabelvåg, Lofoten Islands,

Norway. Enemy alien. Refugee, exile, dad, and a tad hungry. Takes him a while to figure out the scream wasn't a scream. He hears it again. Not human. Not animal. Machine. There's no air raid siren. The scream of an electric saw. Schwitters goes outside and sees up the road there is construction. Beyond the borders of the internment camp, there's a carpenter using the school's electric saw. Schwitters would like to get a closer look at that.

As he returns to the school, he looks up at the dormitory and sees Köln at an open window on the second floor, smoking. They make eye contact, and when Schwitters waves hello Köln bends away and disappears into the room.

Now there's a scrap of paper on the ground that catches Schwitters's eye. He goes and picks it up, and as he does, notices movements on the path through the forest. Not a day has passed and Captain Wicklund is marching a fresh set of refugees toward the Folkehøgskole. But these are not like the refugees aboard the fish boat and they are not headed toward the school but somewhere beyond. He sees their uniforms. Nazis. They shuffle, limp, some are injured, along the path, chained together at the ankles as Wicklund and a number of the local hunters guide them. They've got their rifles pointed at them.

kr 22, 24 ~
kr 8, 70 ~
9 / 04 / 40
Schwitters slips the paper into his pocket.

You're awake, says Wicklund.

I'm always awake. And you, too, Captain? The men shake hands.

No, usually I'm asleep right now. Doesn't matter.

I happened to see you with the prisoners.

Yes. Fallen pilots of the Luftwaffe. They get kept separate. Under lock and guard in one of the other buildings, a grocery and barracks in the farm behind ... All young. Young men. Henk's age. It's a pity a young man's attraction to war.

Yes. And an old man's predilection to send them, says Schwitters. Art revives the lamenting soul. That's what I've always found. Would you like to see ... some sketches? says Schwitters and flips through his book for Wicklund's eyes to impress upon, drawings, colour cartoons quite finished, quick charcoal portraits, splashy watercolour landscapes, lines of poetry: *you won't get a chance to paint / pack real good –* , sketches of the train, the shore, trees, the carpenters.

Sir, I must compliment your drawings. All this in the last two days?

My only desire, Captain, is that I may use the Folkehøgskole's art studios and supplies a little bit.

Of course.

Does that carpenter over there have your electric saw? What a tremendous shriek that monster emits. And portable! What a thing. I love it already and I haven't even laid eyes on it. May I ... take a gander?

Tomorrow, Schwitters. For now, rest.

Oh, no, thank you, Captain, but I don't rest.

Then you could help in the kitchen.

No rest. Not if Köln is awake. If he's sitting at that window and doesn't need rest then neither should Schwitters.

When Schwitters sees some of the children swing open the doors of the gymnasium and run down the steps, he knows a new day has begun. The children have slept and are hungry. After breakfast is served and Schwitters has cleaned up and eaten a plate, maybe that's when he'll rest. Now it's time to do as Wicklund says. And so he goes and scrubs the pots and pans the science teacher needs for the next round of salted fish, beets and leeks, duck eggs, and fried bread to feed the refugees. The enemy aliens. The prisoners. That's what they are. Schwitters knows he's a prisoner but what can he do? The children are eating, their parents are next. The adolescents don't even line up, they run, run and find somewhere to hide. They run around every last inch of the schoolyard and explore what can be explored within boundaries. Schwitters hears them, loud and oblivious to their noise, like cats fighting. They warn each other *don't go past*. They sit on the rocks and stare at the white line. They play at a careful distance. They climb any staircase, doorway, or window; they inspect crevices, locks, pipes, pits, quietly murmuring to themselves. He picks garbage off the ground and puts it in any one of his pockets. The children have been watching him and laugh, they find him even more hilarious on land than at sea, and imitate him behind his back. Excellent imitations. They don't know that Schwitters knows they watch him, and they don't know it's for their entertainment that he acts like such a clown, even when he's alone.

The children watch Schwitters watch the barracks being built down the road in the yard behind the grocer. Schwitters doesn't draw the carpenters, he draws the children. There is tall green grass to run through, wild emmer to chew, spongy moss to jump on, flowers like freckles, and a few gilled mushrooms popping up here and there. On the outcrop there is a lace of white and green lichens, and under the rocks are tiny white centipedes. White as ivory, they hate the light. In groups of three and four and five, the children circle and recircle the grounds. All while they sing the *Ursonate*.

Kwiiee kwiiee kwiiee kwiiee! Kwiiee kwiiee kwiiee kwiiee! Rakete rinnzekete! Rakete rinnzekete!

The Ursonate took Schwitters ten years to compose. His life was very different in 1920 when he began work on the piece. Sturm galerie in Berlin is gone now, liquidated by the Nazis. His gallery in Paris was liquidated as well. The Nazis looted his art with all the rest. Klee, Picasso, Mondrian, Dali, Chagall, Kandinsky, Matisse. Schwitters knew it was time to leave Germany when the Nazis toured their stolen property across the country in a show they called *Degenerate Art*. They hung one of his large Merz collages crooked and upside down, and Hitler had his picture taken in front of it, pointing and smiling open-mouthed like he's laughing, like Hitler's saying, *What is the matter with you, Kurt Schwitters?* After the *Degenerate Art* tour was completed, they burned all the art. What couldn't be burned was smashed to pieces. It's all gone now. They made sure of that. And so are all of the artists, exiled or dead.

Kwiiee kwiiee kwiiee kwiiee. Kwiiee kwiiee kwiiee kwiiee. Rakete rinnzekete! Rakete rinnzekete!

He's got six pockets in his pants, two on his shirt, four on his vest, his sweater has two, no, four pockets, and his overcoat has seven pockets. Enough to lay out a new collage, if he can ever find some glue and a surface.

Henk walks the perimeter and speaks with the guards. There are two men at each station now. One guard is an old man with rosy cheeks and a plum for a nose, a wiry physique and a round belly. He's lugging a double-barrelled shotgun and hunting knife. There's his partner, a tall, equally old man, or older, dressed in black wool, with a narrow face and arms and legs like sticks, a cane in one hand and a pistol in the other. As Schwitters gets a better look at the guards, he can guess from their clothes they are fishermen, loggers, hunters, farmers, and their fathers.

Excuse me, pardon me, says Schwitters as he approaches two of the internment camp guards stationed together down the road from the entrance to the school. The guards stand together, gripping their rifles, talking in a low passionate back-and-forth and looking over at the grocery store where the carpenters are at work. I wonder if you know of any spare *wood* on our grounds. You see, I'm an artist and I'm looking for –

What's the matter with you? Flip off. Can't you see we're busy? They're building barracks for Nazi POWs, mister, so it's high flipping alert. Get back to your dorms if you know what's smart.

Okay but before I go, what about a glue pot? Seen one of those around? Varnish maybe?

I said leave us alone, you old badger. Before I let off rounds.

Henk witnesses the end of this exchange and goes over to reprimand Schwitters and drag him away from the perimeter of the camp borders. What is the matter with you, Schwitters? says Henk loudly so the others can hear. I told you, Schwitters, don't pester the guards. You can see they're on tenterhooks. I'd be worried they're trigger jumpy. The others, Schwitters. Be like the others. The other refugees are content to read or write letters or catch a cold, sleep, eat, while you roam these yards in search of trouble. Look. Between you and me. Not to *me*, but to those who don't *understand* you, well, Schwitters, all this roaming, it makes you look suspicious. Suspicious is a problem for you. It puts your life in danger. Do you understand that's why I'm telling you this?

Thank you, Henk. I appreciate your honesty.

Well, that's because I feel I know you.

I won't interrupt them *ever* again. I was asking if they knew of a few materials, wood and glue, like that, that I needed in order to make a Merz. They told me the carpenters are putting in barracks for POWs.

And walls. And barbed wire. And guards' towers. And what else, Schwitters? They're bringing in POWs. Nazis, Schwitters.

All of a sudden Henks stops in the trail and holds Schwitters where he stands, then shoves him.

What was that for? asks Schwitters.

Oh, and just by the way, that's thanks for telling me about *Köln*. I *asked* you, Schwitters. We were walking together and I asked you. Do you remember?

Yes.

I asked if there were any Nazis aboard and you said you didn't know. Now I hear Köln is an infiltrator.

Henk, I told you I don't know anything. I haven't got a shred of evidence. And you, Henk, you probably have no more proof than me. Someone shared gossip? I don't share suspicions. False allegations can get more than one man killed these days.

We'll find out one way or another. And then he'll be dealt with.

Onboard, Köln helped me cook and clean. When others got sick, he and I washed clothes and dishes, and the floor. He has done nobody any harm. He's quiet. Quiet, that's all.

Fine then. For now. And what is this Merz you invented that I keep hearing about? asks Henk. I thought it was a gadget. Henk is looking Schwitters up and down. Is it … on you? Is this Merz on you? Show it to me.

I told you. Merz is me. Merz is my process and my object. Merz is also bigger than me. Merz is very big.

You're a real broken axle, Schwitters, says Henk. I try to help you. But you make it so hard. You keep going on in the same wrong direction. You're just lucky to be alive, that's all I can say.

I have the materials for a collage.

Schwitters, I don't know what that means, says Henk, but you're probably not allowed to make a collage *here*. This is an enemy alien refugee camp. If you're an artist, why not just paint the horizon line like a normal person.

Collage can *also* be a picture of a place, my friend, Henk. Made up of fragments from here and there, like dabs of paint. I find I have materials and compositions going simultaneously for between three and nine collages.

You lost me, Schwitters.

It's true, Henk. It is easy to get lost with a collage.

Okay, well, I was told in school you had to make it look realistic.

Consider collage, Henk. You might find the medium very rejuvinating.

How did you get me talking about collage, Schwitters? Just go away. You should not be roaming around near the perimeter here. Mind your own business, old man. This isn't some health spa.

That's when Schwitters decides his dorm room is the most suitable place for him if he's going to make a few more drawings, as well as cut, position, and paste what's found here and there. He's gathered some gems. Pulling out of his pockets real memories. The boat rocking passengers. The black on black of Nazi warplanes crossing the night sky overhead while strafing the streets below indiscriminately. The whole Schwitters house reeking of bone glue. Finally it would seem from the way he's travelling so incoherently through time that he's fallen asleep.

Did you hear that, Ernst? Esther, are you awake? Was it shotgun fire?

No, some street or factory noise, Father. Go back to sleep. I'm not tired.

Listen, Ernst. Father's right. Air raid sirens. Quickly, they're shelling us.

Ladies and gentlemen, if you'll please ... thank you, yes ... and now please give a warm *welcome* to the one and the only, as he makes his prodigal return to the Berlin cabaret, the incomparable inventor of Merz, the composer and performer of the notorious *Ursonate*, the epileptic degenerate enemy of the Reich, the Dadaist too Dada for Dada, Hanover's most beloved misfit, modern art's most avant-garde, proud father of an ungrateful child, the boy they used to call dog, now listen for yourselves as he howls in triumph, Kurt Schwitters ...

Fümms bö wö tää zää Uu,

pögiff,

kwii Ee.

Ooooooooooooooooooooooooooo,

dll rrrrr beeeee bö
dll rrrrr beeeee bö fümms bö,
rrrrr beeeee bö fümms bö wö,
beeeee bö fümms bö wö tää,
bö fümms bö wö tää zää,
fümms bö wö tää zää Uu ...

In a field, with Müller-Blensdorf, listening to the echo of a megaphone shouting orders from the top of a pole overlooking the POW barracks up the road. The grass is icy. There's ice on the wildflowers. What day is it? Schwitters is sure it's been a week but Schulz tells him forty-eight hours. Ice in the air glitters like fishscale. The smell of diesel, a dunny cloud over the horizon, out at sea. The sea is a dark marble plane and the snow disappears on it.

Oh, this is some fine predicament. With the devil at our necks, Müller-Blensdorf says, shivering. The devil himself chased us here. Where it's always sunny and always cold. Where you can't tell day from night. And they lock us in right next door to our enemy? The ones sworn to murder us? I must be going mad.

But in the meantime, says Schwitters as he ponderously wipes his nose with his fingers and then wipes his fingers on his shirt collar, I wonder if I might find a glue pot.

You must be mad already. He spits. And anyhow *the figure* is the core to the artist's craft, the only true test of an artist's ability.

It's nice to see you back on your feet, Müller-Blensdorf. Now, after some rest and some food, I recognize the vigorous man I met back at the train station in Molde. Reminds me, how are your children?

That's kind of you, says Müller-Blensdorf as he lights the cigarette he's kept tucked behind his ear until now. He inhales, exhales, then takes a second drag. They miss their mother, of course, he says. I'm not … she just … I don't know, Schwitters. You saw. She just leaped from the train … I don't know why … what do I *say* when the children ask me? They keep asking me, Schwitters. It's breaking me. I don't *know* if she's alive. How am I supposed to raise our children alone? I'm on the verge of collapse. Our life is all gone, vanished, like a coin trick. My poor pitiable poor innocent children. What shall I do with them?

Take good, good care of them, says Schwitters. Stay cheerful. Be stupid. Be an idiot. For them. But be smart for them. And protect them. But these are horrible times and they need you to make them laugh … they need you *more* than you need your wife. If you can imagine that.

Müller-Blensdorf quietly sobs.

The two artists watch as their friend Schulz makes his way across the green toward them. He holds something small that sparkles, which he delicately turns over in his fingers, fawning over it.

What's he *got* there? says Müller-Blensdorf through a kerchief.

Perhaps an angel, Schwitters says. Looks like an angel.

Angels are much bigger, don't you know? Bigger than us.

Kwiiee kwiiee kwiiee kwiiee! Kwiiee kwiiee kwiiee kwiiee! says Schulz.

Rakete rinnzekete! Rakete rinnzekete! answer Schwitters and Müller-Blensdorf.

How are you, Müller-Blensdorf? You look sick.

I'm fine. I'll be good in a moment.

Schwitters, I found this, says Schulz. For your collage. Seeing it reminded me of the night we arrived, when you called the sun by her Norse name. He hands Schwitters a crinkled piece of silver and red foil. A candy wrapper with the word *Freia* printed in calligraphy on it.

Thank you so much, Schulz, what a very meaningful gesture, says Schwitters and he slips the foil into the inside breast pocket of his overcoat.

I also found this, Schulz says and hands him a flat wood disc, painted blue, with a hole in the middle.

Lovely. The end of a spool, says Schwitters as he rubs his thumb against it. But hold on. Night we arrived, you say. Well how long have we been here now? I seem to have lost track.

You *lost track*, Schwitters? says Schulz with absolute shock. How is that *possible*? My god. Haven't you heard? The war is *twenty miles* from us. We'll be leaving soon. You're oblivious. Now, see, they put up butcher paper over all the windows in the schoolhouse and dormitory so no one can see in or out. We won't be here much longer.

Yes, but how long have we been here?

Schulz whispers so both men can hear him. So word around the dorms is that Köln isn't a Nazi at all. Surpised? You haven't heard this yet? Köln is not a Nazi. He's a Romeo. Apparently in his interrogation with Wicklund he confessed he was the lover of that young and famous wealthy debutante ace female pilot who broke all the world's aviation records, Gidsken Jakobsen.

That's absurd, says Müller-Blensdorf and spits.

What do you think of that, Schwitters? Romeo or Nazi?

… Why not both? Or neither?

You're so agnostic, Schwitters, I could strangle you, says Müller-Blensdorf.

No going back. No idea what lies ahead. This island is all there is right now. And these people. Nothing else to hang on to. No reason to mark out the calendar and make a schedule. On an undesirable journey with no certain end. The war races toward them. Clocks matter less. Internment is asynchronous. When the refugees don't have something to distract them, like Schwitters's songs and pantomimes, or Esther's dancing, or the science teacher's meals, fear tramples in and great waves of anxiety shut so many of them down. They can't concentrate. Can't form complete sentences or follow a coherent line of thought. Forgetful. Dozy, half-lidded, distracted. The refugees seem to have lost bits and pieces of their will to live. A month of running, the trials of exile have chipped away at the weak spots of their psyche. Either they are resigned to their fate or mentally incapable of the same daily practicality that once made them functioning members of society. Schwitters would like to tell them all: Wake up! But that would be hypocritical of Schwitters since he would very much like to fall asleep.

Later in the morning, possibly mid-afternoon, or evening, but just as Schwitters is about to fall asleep, he senses Köln. He rises from his cot. Immediately, he runs, with sketch pad and pencils, down the stairs and out the front door of the dorms to the nearest view of the grounds. Müller-Blensdorf's children wake at the sound of his jacket and its contents and follow him and then are chased back to bed by their father. So they look out the window of their dorm room and see Köln, of all people, out for a walk. How did he know? the children want to know. How did he know Köln would be up? Their father has no idea. The family watches Köln walk the perimeter of the camp alone, before he's suddenly interrupted.

Kwiiee kwiiee kwiiee kwiiee! Kwiiee kwiiee kwiiee kwiiee! sings Schwitters. Köln, I thought I might find you out here. Who can sleep under this midnight sun?

Köln stares at him.

Yes, but before I go. Do know any tradecrafts, Köln? You see, Wicklund plans to open the carpentry studio. And he's promised a demonstration of his electric circular saw ... Picture this, my friend. The blade is circular. Spins faster than an airplane propeller. Cuts through a plank in mere seconds.

No answer.

We're a world away from Berlin, aren't we? How far do you have to go before you'll feel free to speak your mind, Köln? You know, they're all wretched. Nothing pure about the Reich. I knew Goebbels over twenty years ago from cabarets where we all drank and I sometimes recited poems and fairy tales. Skinny man like a piece of broken fence draped in a stinky suit. Very strong body odour. Ever see Goebbels up close? Rank man. All the artists knew him before '33. He was such a vile critic. Nobody liked him. And he hated everyone. What was he doing there? He used to skulk in the shadows of the artists' bars all over Germany listening in to conversations and then printing his counter-opinions in his magazine, *Der Angriff*. Eventually he stopped showing his face around after George Grosz published a caricature of him in London's *Times Literary Supplement*. But this one night in Dessau, though, I remember he spent *billions* buying me and Hannah Höch schnapps. Oh, he toasted my performance, yes. Here's to the *Ursonate*. Then shouted out how he *despised it*. Decadent to the core. He loved shoving his sweaty money in our faces. Then listen to this, Köln, this was the kind of joke we would tell. Once I remember Goebbels asked if I would, in the future, make more of an effort to emulate the great Romantic poet, Heinrich von Kleist, who, he was keen to remind me, took his own life at the age of thirty-four.

No response from Köln.

It must have been in '25 or '26, coming across a streetwalker no older than fifteen, who promised us she would be our slave for an hour, for only six billion marks and a cigarette. And who do you guess she went with? Who threw money at the girl and dragged her off?

Silence.

Goebbels. Yes. There was a time when I read closely the works of Spinoza and Schopenhauer. We could discuss their ideas, you and I, Köln. Would you study with me the great works of philosophy? If not the library, perhaps the carpentry studio interests you?

I'll see the studio. Later. Now go, says Köln in a little reedy voice and the accent of a born Berliner.

That accent, when hears it, really takes Schwitters back to a world he hasn't heard from in years. That Berliner street dog diphthong, those shadow-lurking noises like the wet courtyards and stinking stairwells, all inside Köln's German. Almost nostalgia for Schwitters, almost.

I'll see the studio. Later. Now go.

Collecting collecting collecting. Gathering gathering gathering. Finding finding finding. Cutting cutting cutting. Gluing gluing gluing.

Amazing, says Schwitters to himself. Amazing amazing amazing, he says as he makes his way down the dormitory hall toward his room. His heart pounds, hands are clammy. What a day, what a night, what an occasion. This is cause for celebration. Köln spoke. Seven words. Incredible. Like seven clean slaps across the face, hearing him speak like that.

I'll see the studio. Later. Now go, Schwitters writes it on a piece of his sketching paper. *Köln speaks!*

The Merz he keeps in his pocket grows smoother by the day. Now a dappled white semi-orb, he gently sands away all trace of the stone's original edges. Turned inward like a mother's hip. With child, that's how he imagines the red-painted found wood he's tied inside the stone's natural curve with umbilical wires.

Spring in Kabelvåg, a sketch in charcoal on found paper. Sun and moon share the sky. Thickly cross-hatched clouds hang like wasps' nests over the Lofoten Islands. The horizon is a jagged black line of mountains and valleys. The ocean is a marbled slab. *Watch out for the Luftwaffe!* he scribbles underneath. Next page. His wife, Helma, back at home in Hanover. How he wishes he was there with her. He likes drawing her face and shading her plump cheeks. *Take care of the Merzbau!* he writes. Next page. Schwitters draws the night of his escape from Lysaker with Ernst and Esther, and he draws the eternal night, and he draws the night on the cold docks in Tromsø where they joined so many other refugees fleeing north. And where they first met Köln.

Satisfied with his efforts, Schwitters is once again off to see his son and daughter-in-law in their dorm. As he figured, they are in bed resting. Ernst has an arm over his eyes to block out the light. Esther is sitting on the edge of the cot darning a moth-hole in her skirt but doesn't look unhappy to see her father-in-law. Right away Schwitters wants to talk about Wicklund's promise to open the carpentry studio and how delighted he is at this prospect. He gets an affirming nod from Esther. Ernst doesn't move. So then Schwitters can't help but mention what he really came here about, the really big news that Köln *spoke* for the first time. Seven words. What a breakthrough! Of course there's nothing Schwitters can do to stir his son.

Not everyone feels like talking all the time, says Ernst. You should try it.

Father, Esther says, don't be foolish.

To be expected. With no support from them, Schwitters returns to the dormitory's main floor foyer where he finds Captain Wicklund wandering in circles, holding a baby bottle and a flannel blanket. The captain's chin is raised, his head flicks side to side, like a man deep in a daydream, so that it would seem to Schwitters the old headmaster is lost on his own little inner campus.

I was just looking for you, Captain, says Schwitters.

Ah, Schwitters. Can you help me? The couple with the ten-month-old? Wicklund says. Do you know where they are? They are supposed to be waiting right here. I brought this from a … nurse.

You mean the Hallbauers.

The Hallbauers, yes, that's the name.

Warm milk for the baby? I can take this to them.

If you would, I'd be very grateful, says Wicklund, thank you. I can't even remember their faces.

The mother's not exactly Gidsken Jakobsen, is she?

No, no, I suppose she isn't? Why do you say?

Perhaps while I find them, *you* could open the arts and crafts studio as you mentioned? I was just talking about it with my son and daughter, who seemed overjoyed at the prospect of a craft to distract them from this despair.

Wicklund looks as if he's about to speak but then doesn't. He stares at Schwitters.

Schwitters reminds him. On our first night here, you told me –

Yes, our conversation –

Yes, and then again some time later you repeated how pleased you were that so many artists were interned here and how happy you'd be for us to use your school's carpentry studio and its supplies.

I remember, Schwitters, I remember. All right. Yes, I did. The arrival of the POWs shouldn't disadvantage you. And of course I always honour my word. What I'll do is send over a guard. I'll send Henk. You and a few others may use the tools. Just don't abuse my trust. Be sensible. We are in wartimes.

And if I can still take you up on the offer of the demonstration on your electrical saw, I'd be delighted, says Schwitters.

Wicklund checks the time on his silver fob. In an hour I will provide a demonstration of the electrical circular saw.

Circular, you say? I forget if I knew that already. Well, of course it's a circle, like a wheel, that does sound fascinating, absolutely fascinating, says Schwitters.

You're an authentic, Schwitters, says Wicklund as he wedges one boot out the front door of the dormitory. You don't think of anything but art. Not politics. Not rest. Not even war distracts you. Trust me, Schwitters, even after so many years as principal of an arts and crafts school, I can still recognize the purity of your devotion. You're a very genuine and pure individual, this I believe.

That's very kind of you, Captain. My devotion is to Merz, he says. Merz, Merz, and Merz. Schwitters waves the hot milk bottle to and fro. As you see, Captain, in the eyes of the Master Race, though, my devotion makes me a degenerate. I'm a poison the Reich wants out of their system. Exile the impure artist, or better yet kill him! And that, dear Captain, that is my authentic fate.

Let's both pray things change for the better soon.

Kwiiee kwiiee kwiiee kwiiee! Kwiiee kwiiee kwiiee kwiiee!

The men shake hands and say goodbye and off Schwitters goes to deliver the hot bottle to the Hallbauers. It is easy for him to find the family. If they are not in the foyer, and not in their dorm, the Hallbauers are in the bathroom with their infant.

Kwiiee kwiiee kwiiee kwiiee. Kwiiee kwiiee kwiiee kwiiee, says Schwitters as he approaches the dorm room's open door.

Rakete rinnzekete. Rakete rinnzekete, Rachel Hallbauer answers, and takes the warm milk bottle from Schwitters and puts it to the child's mouth.

Kwiiee kwiiee kwiiee kwiiee. Kwiiee kwiiee kwiiee kwiiee, says Schwitters.

Rakete rinnzekete. Rakete rinnzekete, answers the first refugee.

Bö fö böwö fümmsbö böwörö fümmsböwö, says Gert Hallbauer.

What did you do today? asks Schwitters.

Gert waves his arms in the air, I didn't get out of this cot. Some influenza.

And *you*?

Rachel says, Me, too. I'm sick, too. Only the baby remains healthy, thank God. I didn't get out of bed until just now. This is the most I've slept uninterrupted in more than a month. What did you do today, Schwitters?

Well, poetry, foraging, finding, familiarizing, plus modest stomach pains. And I just spoke with Captain Wicklund. He's promised to open up the carpentry studio and let us use the tools. Would either of you like to join me?

Gert's not interested. He says he's heard there are *twenty-three* Nazis locked in that grocery store up the road. God forbid, is that true, Schwitters? Gert asks.

On my reconnoiter I counted twenty-five. But, the good news is that we shall get a demonstration of the school's *electric* saw. I heard of it when we first arrived. A blade fixed in some manner so you can hold it while it does the cutting all by itself, apparently. Also a pottery studio. A painting studio. A photography studio, too, which my son Ernst Blendorf is sure to find of interest. There is a black-and-white darkroom, *and* a colour darkroom. All this up here in the Arctic Circle. Who would have thought? Do either of you work in the arts?

Who can think about *art* when the world is on fire? At least the cod boat was on the *move*. I find all this *Dragestil* architecture oppressive, don't you, Schwitters?

I don't know, Hallbauer, it has its charm.

The ocean. It's huge. That's better. We're easy pickings here on this small, stupid rock. And we're double-trapped.

You of all people want to get back on a boat. My dear Gert, says Schwitters. Sick the moment we left the dock.

Look around, Schwitters. Haven't you noticed? This fence

they're building is not for *our* safety, it's to reassure the villagers, obviously. They're afraid of *us*. We're in prison. What if the Nazis break free of the POW camp up the road, then what do we do? We're readymade corpses. What if the Nazis invade in full force? We die. By their hands. Or our own.

You're a father, says Schwitters.

Suicide is our *only* choice.

I'd rather die by my own hand, says Rachel.

The baby in her arms drinks quietly from the bottle.

Yes, but *how*? asks her husband. What *means* do we have? Our *bare* hands? Strangle each other? Leap out the windows? It's not really high enough. The chances of living are too great. There's nothing here to kill ourselves with. Just wood and linens. Is that enough?

Oh, there's *got* to be something, says Schwitters. You just have to know how to *look*.

Always the optimist, says Rachel.

Yes, Schwitters, take your eyes off the trash for a minute and find us a way, a humane way to go …, says Gert.

The children fall out of their bunks and race each other to the deck of the fishing boat to watch the fireworks. Schwitters holds three of them under his coat. Another three huddle in a blanket. Round after round of British pilots rout the enemy in the sky and drown them and their aircraft in the ocean. The Nazi warship that's been following them suddenly lights up on the horizon. One explosion and then another and another as the whole great boat explodes, and a few seconds later, as the refugees are cheering, a thunderous shockwave knocks a few kids off their feet and makes the younger ones cry out in fear. The fishing boat rocks a bit. It's okay, kids, it's over. The chase is over. We're safe for now, Schwitters says and hugs them tight. Meanwhile a huge plume of fiery black smoke gathers in the sky over the carcass of the Nazi ship. A dark, toxic mushroom cloud filled with its own lightning and falling ashen debris. And then, after all the danger has passed, Schwitters begins to tremble. He takes a deep breath and commands his body to stop shaking. Let's drink that champagne *now*, says Schulz and everyone agrees. Even the boat's captain has a glass. He looks so tired.

fümmsböwötääzääUu pöggiff
fümmes bö wö tää zää Uu,
pöggiff,
kwiiee
kwiiee
kwiiee
kwiiee
kwiiee
kwiiee

Dedesnn nn rrrrr,
        Ii Ee,
          mpiff tillff toooo,
Dedesnn nn rrrrr,
    desnn nn rrrrr
      nn nn rrrrr
      nn rrrrr

Henk stands against the door of the studio, holding it open as he writes the name down in his book of everyone who enters. With his rifle prominent, his eyes down in his book, no word of hello, Henk has shed a lot of his earlier gentleness and has battened down inside a harder self. As Schwitters makes his grand entrance, he bows as he passes Henk and says, Thank you, my dear friend Henk, good day or good evening, whichever it is. How *are* you? They say the louder you talk the closer they get.

I don't know why *he* lets you enemy aliens *in* here, says Henk.

My name is Kurt Schwitters.

You know what your name is? Suspect. You're no different to me than the men locked up at the grocery store.

Henk, don't let your first whiff of war turn you against all your better instincts.

Get your claws off me, you old badger. Go use the tools. You won't be here long enough to do more than whittle a few chunks.

No, Henk, with every breath I make art, says Schwitters as he takes in the view. All the tools hung on the wall! The multiple woodworking tables. The aromatic stacks of woodblock in the corner. The philosopher, Schulz, is already seated at one table with a good piece of spruce, chiselling. Turns out the Hallbauers did decide to come by, and brought their child with them to see what's available in the adjoining painting studio. There's also a pottery studio beyond a set of double doors, where Schwitters sees Müller-Blensdorf examining his options. At the other end of the woodworking studio, to his right, there are glazed doors that open into a photography studio that Ernst and Esther have already begun inspecting for its different cameras, lenses, and darkroom equipment.

But Schwitters doesn't see the one object he was most hoping would be here. The electrical saw.

Did the captain tell you when he would provide his demonstration? I don't see the electrical saw anywhere.

It's right over there, Schwitters, says Henk and he points with his chin to an empty table in the far corner by the cabinets.

Schwitters's eyes light up. Ah! Well. As I've heard it said, *Go where the fish jump.*

Shut up and make your art then, says Henk.

Yes, there it is. On a table of its own, polished clean as a new passport, is the machine Schwitters has thought so much about these last few days interned here, the electrical circular saw. He's got at most five steps to reach the machine but he needs to catch his balance on his way. He feels top-heavy. Suddenly he's aware of how empty his stomach is, and how long it's been since he had a good rest. Not since shells fell on Oslo. But he has the saw all to himself now. It's just Schwitters and the electrical saw. And he is completely stunned. It's so beautiful. Quietly seated there on the table with its long thick cord wrapped in a coil behind like a strange web it's spinning. It's a giant jewel, a shining contortion, a dazzling ornament fit for a queen. A sleek machine. It's got a leather-padded handle welded to the back of its polished steel shell, and doesn't look more than ten pounds all told. Like some strange kind of imaginary sea predator. A silver, armoured mollusc with an exposed mouth filled with dozens of intimately serrated teeth. It's a mesmerizing object. Schwitters can't take his eyes off it. It's love at first sight. How its sleek and smooth exterior cradles this deadly sharp blade, and how that blade, thin as a piece of Bristol board, is able to spin at unthinkable speeds on an unbreakable axle. Why does the circular electrical saw make him so want to weep? The saw is as perfect as a piece of art, like one of Arp's contours, like one of Höch's collages, like a whorl peeled off a Picabia painting, like a shiny child designed by Boccioni, but no, no, not Arp not Höch not Picabia not Boccioni, no! Rakete rinnzekete! Rakete rinnzekete! ... it's a Merz. He's looking at a Merz. He's *found* a Merz. Sign it Kurt Schwitters. He wishes he could bring it back to Helma in Hanover and put it in the Merzbau he built inside their home at Waldhausenstrasse 5. And no doubt it would fit perfectly! Wouldn't that be wonderful? What an ideal addition to his Merzbau. He misses Helma and Waldhausenstrasse 5 terribly, he misses Helma, he misses the Merzbau, he misses Hanover, Berlin, and Hannah Höch. As he stares in pitiful awe at the sublime contours and bitter sharpness of the electric saw, Schwitters thinks if Henk were in a better mood, he would touch it.

While distracted with his ogling, Schwitters doesn't notice Esther has come up beside him with a Kodak on a tripod. She asks to take his picture and that's when he notices her and his son. He's delighted to see the Kodak. However, Ernst carries nothing more than a look of pained chagrin.

The photographer has lost his passion, says Schwitters of his boy.

How can you think of art at a time like this?

But look, aren't we in paradise, Ernst? Look at all the supplies. What else should I think about? I hope we live out the war here.

This is all ripe for Nazi plunder, says Ernst. I'm going to go find some wood to make my coffin.

What about the darkroom? Have you taken a look inside? Do they have all the chemicals and plates necessary?

Oh, I'm not going to *use* the darkroom, Ernst laughs. It's a cute facility full of valuable equipment I'm sure the Nazis will enjoy. It's been a nice tour and now I'm actually going back to bed.

But wait, Ernst, wait. Help your wife take some pictures of the electric saw for me? asks Schwitters. I absolutely need *some* documentation of it.

A rare electric saw, Ernst sighs as he massages his temples. Ground-breaking, incredibly desirable technology, right here, *locked up with us*. My chest, my sinuses – why would I take a photograph? I can barely *see*. I can't focus my *mind*. How am I going to focus a camera?

Alone at another table where he's been carving, Schulz all of a sudden lets out a giant sob and puts his forehead down on the table.

Ernst is silent. Then Esther begins crying. Schwitters is looking at the electric saw and how its silky shine resembles wet skin.

Why do I want to *blame you* for this, too, Schwitters? says Ernst.

For *what*, my dear? For our good luck?

Good luck? Ernst laughs. For the tears, man! The tears! Ernst flaps his arms around. What's the matter with this picture? We're all damned to hell.

You blame me *for the war*? My son, *that's* hardly fair.

It *is* fair, you fool. It's not the landscape painter who got us into trouble. It's Merz! Merz got us here. It's the decadence and degeneracy of *your entire generation* the Nazis reacted against. The Nazis hate *you*. And all of the decadent, *degenerate*

German artists of your whole entire generation. *You, Schwitters.* You are always named among the leaders of your era. In effect, Hitler is rallying against *you*. You *are* to blame.

Well, that's flattering, Ernst, but – I know you're being facetious.

At first it looks as if Ernst going to pick up the electric circular saw and throw it at him or smash it into Schwitters's head, but then his son veers toward the exit. He's gone.

Ernst – , calls out Esther. But he's already past Henk and out the door.

I can't tell who he hates more, me or Hitler.

Oh, Papa, that's not true, says Esther. Don't think that. He adores you. Idolizes you. Didn't you hear him talking about you, how famous you are? *But you know Ernst.* He needs to be his *own* man. He hates to be seen as *weak* in front of you. And yet, he's so weak.

Ernst is proud of his many weaknesses because the Reich hates any sign of weakness. What can I do, he always feels he's in competition with his older brother, Merz. Merz is created from the discards of German society. And he feels Germany discarded him. Because Merz is German refuse and he is German refuse, he struggles.

Yes, I know, Papa. He calls Merz his famous older brother. He loves Merz. He knows every one of your poems by heart. But his feelings are mixed up. Admiration that's also jealousy.

Everything I do is for Ernst. Merz is *for* Ernst. Even though Merz came first, Merz springs from the desire for Ernst. Before Ernst, there was no Merz. Baby Ernst inspired Merz. I've told him this fact so many times. He's all I have. Without him, there is no Merz. Merz is just my portrait of Ernst.

Henk opens the front doors again and a fierce gust off the sea almost yanks the knob from his hand. It's liable to blow your hat off if you don't hold it on, says Captain Wicklund as he rushes inside.

My father says a storm is due, Henk tells the captain. He doesn't right away shut the door, though, because Ernst has decided to come sulking back into the studio so he can also watch the demonstration. His hair is ruined by the wind. And the side of his jacket is muddy, from what he explains to Esther and Schwitters was the result of getting blown over by intense winds.

Then another refugee arrives. Köln. Henk nods to him and says, Take a seat somewhere, the show's just about to begin.

Köln doesn't speak to anyone but he makes his way through the woodworking shop until he's all the way around and seated at a table back near the doors. Schulz and Müller-Blensdorf sit at one table while the Hallbauers and their baby occupy another.

Captain Wicklund stands behind the electric saw and waits until everyone is settled before he begins his demonstration. He puts his hands on the steel and caresses the shell then grips the handle firmly. Our new electrical saw only arrived in January, says the captain. I feel a little like a new father, her guardian and protector, he says with a laugh. The effort to acquire her took the greater part of a year, Wicklund goes on to tell those gathered. Much correspondence, long negotiations. Captain Wicklund plugs the cord connected to the saw into a generator that's fixed to the floor nearby. Wicklund claims it is the first of its kind in all of Norway, this electrical saw.

Just wait until I turn it on, he says and hits the trigger.

When Wicklund switches on the power and the saw screams alive, the whole room startles. Some leap back. Some jolt upright or hop off the floor. Schwitters almost doubles over in surprise. Even Köln, who sometimes appears made of solid stone, bounces off his feet. A dragon. A screaming, hissing dragon. The saw is so loud. Deafeningly loud. The loudest musical instrument Schwitters has ever heard. He's completely delighted. All he wants in the world is to take the saw home and make it his own.

The sound is so audacious, the Hallbauer baby bursts into tears and the family is up and on their feet, rushing past Henk, looking very cross at the captain as they leave the studio so they can soothe their bawling, terrified infant.

Under his safety goggles, Wicklund can't see the family leave. He's flushed bright red as he announces loudly that he's about to start cutting. A big smile on his face, and the saw steadily screaming, the blade spinning so fast it looks motionless. Wicklund prepares the electric circular saw over a slab of plankwood. He releases the safety lock on the shield and lifts it away from the blade, then levels the wood on the table. The saw howls at a dizzying, high pitch as its steel teeth spin at an electrified ultraspeed straight through the wood. Sawdust as fine as mist rises around the captain. The blade slides right in. What a thrill, Schwitters says as Wicklund cuts a sober line with ferocious precision and in what must be less than ten seconds. Wicklund takes his finger off the trigger, and while the blade continues to spin down, Wicklund shows off the astonishing work it did on the plank. An absolutely clean edge. Schwitters applauds. He can't even hear his own hands clapping.

Just as Wicklund is about to speak, Köln steps in front, and with a single bearpaw of a hand squeezing Wicklund's face, Köln pushes the captain aside. Wicklund falls, hits his ear on the corner of a cabinet, and collapses on the ground.

Köln looks straight at Schwitters. Remember me, he says. Remember me when you see your enemy again, says Köln and he picks up the saw, triggers the engine, puts his head on the table, and with all his strength, pushes the blade down on his skull.

There's a terrible noise and after an excruciating explosion, Köln spins away, falls to the ground, and the electric saw follows him. Blood, the whole studio is covered in a fine mist of it. The walls are all sprayed. The tools, the machinery, the wood and other equipment. Their clothes. The clothes they are wearing are covered. Their faces. Everyone is spattered in it. The electric circular saw is still plugged in but when its blade hit the floor, it took a huge chunk of the wood, which went flying and almost hit Schulz in the head but stopped the saw from spinning. Köln is writhing slowly on the floor now inching closer to Wicklund, who is just coming to after blacking out.

Schwitters bends down and picks up Köln and rests his head in his lap. Someone give me a cloth or anything. Esther knows what to do. Everyone else is standing there, stunned. Run, Ernst, run, my son, and fetch a doctor, Schwitters says, as he wraps a window curtain Esther has supplied around Köln's head. His skull is torn open and shattered and blood quickly soaks the cloth.

He's still alive, Schwitters tells the others.

Köln's eyes are grey and unfocused. But he speaks. You again, Schwitters? We met before the war.

Köln, my friend. After all this time, now you tell me. When was it?

I punched you in the face at a bar in Berlin.

Yes, I remember you now, Köln. It was while I performed the *Ursonate*. I received a standing ovation after you ran away. You're an infamous unnamed villain in the annals of the avant-garde, my friend. I forgive you.

That's kind of you, Schwitters, you prick, but it won't make any difference. And then Köln's eyes fall shut and he's dead.

He's dead, Schwitters tells everybody.

Oh my god, Captain Wicklund says, and gives up trying to stand, slides down the wall, turns his head, bends over, and retches.

Henk starts shouting for everyone to clear out, get out of here, now, he shouts, but it takes a while for any of the refugees to notice his voice, and when they begin to collect themselves and leave, that's just when Ernst arrives back again with a doctor, who stops in the doorway and stares at the body on the floor and then at the state of the studio and almost faints.

Is he dead? Ernst asks from the door. He doesn't want to take another step inside.

Yes, says Schwitters, he's dead. Schwitters gets up gently and rests Köln's head on the floor. He looks at Köln once more there at his feet before going to stand beside his son. He spoke to me, says Schwitters.

What did he...?

He confessed. He confessed everything.

Ernst shakes his head. A fucking Nazi this whole time.

Henk overhears and cries out: A Nazi! I knew it! A goddamn Nazi.

Schwitters looks at Henk and replies with solemnity: Yes, my friend. And to the bitter end.

rakete rinnzekete
rakete rinnzekete
rakete rinnzekete
rakete rinnzekete
rakete rinnzekete
rakete rinnzekete
Beeeee
bö
bö
bö
bö
bö
bö
böwö
böwö
böwö
böwö
böwö
böwö
böwörö
böwörö
böwörö
böwörö
böwörö
böwörö
böwöböpö
böwöböpö

böwöböpö
böwöböpö
böwöböpö
böwöböpö
böwöröböpö
böwöröböpö
böwöröböpö
böwöröböpö
böwöröböpö
böwöröböpö
böwörötääböpö
böwörötääböpö
böwörötääböpö
böwörötääböpö
böwörötääböpö
böwörötääböpö
böwörötääböpö
böwörötääzääböpö
böwörötääzääböpö
böwörötääzääböpö
böwörötääzääböpö
böwörötääzääböpö
böwörötääzääböpö
böwörötääzääUu böpö
böwörötääzääUu böpö
böwörötääzääUu böpö
böwörötääzääUu böpö
böwörötääzääUu böpö
böwörötääzääUu böpö
böwörötääzääUu pögö

böwörötääzääUu pögö
böwörötääzääUu pögö
böwörötääzääUu pögö
böwörötääzääUu pögö
böwörötääzääUu pögö
böwörötääzääUu pögiff
böwörötääzääUu pögiff
böwörötääzääUu pögiff
böwörötääzääUu pögiff
böwörötääzääUu pögiff
böwörötääzääUu pögiff
fümmsböwötääzääUu pögiff
fümmsböwötääzääUu pögiff
fümmsböwötääzääUu pögiff
fümmsböwötääzääUu pögiff
fümmsböwötääzääUu pögiff
fümmes bö wö tää zää Uu,
pögiff,
kwiiee
kwiiee
kwiiee
kwiiee
kwiiee
kwiiee.

This is not the first time someone has looked at Schwitters like that. He left Germany to get away from that look. A look as if to say: What's the matter with you, Schwitters?

From the scene at the studio, Henk escorts the whole group back to the dormitory building where they change out of their bloody clothes, wash their hands and faces in the sink, and wash their clothes and hang them on the line to dry. Perhaps an hour passes. Then Henk is back and walking down the halls of each floor of the dormitory shouting demands. Everyone pack their belongings. The wet stuff, well, that's too bad, but it's up to you, pack it or leave it. The enemy aliens are leaving. As soon as they're ready, the refugees are lined up again in the same building with the classrooms where they were brought upon arrival. For it seems Köln's death has expedited a process that was already underway for transporting the refugees off the island. As Schwitters stands in queue with the others, they learn from Captain Wicklund what is going on.

Despite the mild concussion Köln gave him, Captain Wicklund is back on his feet and rather lucid. He explains that a British officer has commandeered Captain Wicklund's former headmaster's office and is using it just as Wicklund did, to conduct interrogations of each refugee. So long as their papers and answers are satisfactory, the British are taking command of them.

Goodbye, and good fortunes, says Captain Wicklund. But he says it not without passion, and he slurs a little. One eye seems distracted.

It's a pity, says Schwitters and he shakes the captain's hand, that we can't take you with us, Wicklund.

I'll always remember you, Schwitters, says Captain Wicklund drowsily.

Yes, Captain, I know you will.

When Schwitters and the others first arrived at the Vågan Folkehøgskole here in Kabelvåg, this little village on the beak of the Lofoten Islands, flying the Norwegian Sea, he told the gentle and kind Captain Wicklund everything he could about himself, all he could remember and as honestly as he could speak it. Where was he a year ago? A month ago? Who was he with? In the attic of his son's house in Lysaker, sharing a breakfast of cooked cauliflower with his pet mice. His flour and water paste was well stirred and ready for a collage. That's when he saw out of the attic window the city of Oslo light up on the horizon and shockwaves rattled his son's little house all the way out here in Lysaker. Then Nazi paratroopers began falling, some right into Lysaker. Soon there was open fire in the streets and screaming. Machine guns strafed the walls of Ernst and Esther's home. They fled, Schwitters, son, daughter-in-law, identity papers, a pocket-sized sculpture, some pencils, what else. They took the last train north. The plan was to live inside a Merz Schwitters had built over the past seven summers, an inhabitable Merz, constructed out on a deserted island in the Arctic Circle, near Tromsø. He and his son and daughter-in-law spent two weeks in Tromsø interned next to the train station at an empty hotel, ten refugees to a room. The only heat was the stove. Every day Schwitters went and applied for permission to live out the war in his isolated Merz. Schwitters explained that for years now, every summer, he and his wife, his son and his son's wife, had all gone to spend the summers living in the Merz. The Merz was his second home. But they were not granted the right, not even to paddle out to the Merz on the deserted island and hide there for the war. Because it said on his papers he was epileptic, and because he was a German citizen. It didn't make any difference that his son and daughter-in-law were Norwegian citizens. Instead the war sent them to Moen, to Grov, to Drag. In the never-ending shuffle of internments, and nowhere to call home, the war steadily approaching. Norway's own government was about to flee the country. The Nazis were on the ground. A sympathetic codfisherman and his first mate brought as many aboard as he could, and hid them from Nazi warships by skirting down the coastline in lousy weather. There's a hero. Just to save a few people. And here we are in Kabelvåg. That's what Schwitters will say.

It's June of 1940. It's a bright, beautiful evening. The pool of sky Schwitters can see through the window of the interrogation room is such a rich blue he could almost jump out and swim in it. The British officer looks up from his papers at the man across Wicklund's desk from him and says: Name, please.

Dissolving Views

Emily Anglin

For Ellie and Matt.

In the sunlight, the river behind my building was a rushing channel of broken, brown-green glass, dazzling the eye as it rolled. It was six months since I'd last heard from Amber, my twin sister, and I sat alone in my rented condo gazing out at the water, thinking about her. An envelope with information about my severance pay was clutched in one hand and my phone in the other, as though holding these objects would help me think through the present problem: Amber had stopped talking to me and I didn't understand why. It was as though she had begun a new life without me in it.

My patterns of thought had become strange as I'd tried to sort it out; the best way I can explain it is that my every thought felt like it was interrupted halfway through by silence. This mental state, mingled with the hazy environment of the summertime riverside – the plants and birds, and the drone of cicadas – had brought on a torpor I wanted to fight off before it closed like a dome around me.

Other humans were scarce, or so it seemed to me as I hung around there every day by the water. I would walk outside in the mornings with my cup of coffee, the trailing belt of my bathrobe snagging on the bouquet-like clouds of asters and prickling thistles.

Just that morning, I'd felt the too-comfortable haze settling in again. I'd been sitting on the bank, alternately writing in my notebook and watching the water. When I looked back down at my notebook where it sat open in my lap and began to read, alarm sobered me. It was like drinking alcohol in reverse: clarity flowing like a cooling liquid through the blood.

It's always been summer, the entry began. *They tell me that this building was once a school. But, for as long as anyone can* remember, it's been condos. Every person who lives here is always gone, except me. Some of them have never lived here. They just own or rent the empty space. There have never been actual voices, just written words: no faces, skin, hair, or touch, just pictures. I've never worked – never gone to work in a building in the city every day. What matters, what lives, feels, and moves, are the plants that grow outside by the water. Even in the city, the vegetation has grown so long and unruly that surely a tipping point has arrived: now, it will always keep growing; the entanglements of wildflowers, weeds, and invasive vines along the river can only grow more complex, imposs-ible to cut apart from each other, locked into prolonged life by their combined tendrils that conspire, in a kind of union, to forge grafted, interspecies networks.

This, I thought, is not what I should be spending my time on. Any more of it, and I'd be ready for a reclusive life, not unlike our Uncle Paul after he got back from his service as a war photographer: alone, suspicious, blinds drawn, twenty years' worth of days spent in shadow and solitude, all the photos on his walls depicting things and places, not people. Maybe it ran in our family. There was a term for it: *anti-social behaviour*. And a label: *recluse*. No, I thought. No, that's not right. I am not anti-social.

Nor did I have the excuse of any war tours for this strange behaviour. I stood up suddenly, actually shaken. I went inside and sat on the couch.

Maybe it was just that I didn't really like to think about what had happened or where I'd been before this lonely, ourdoor world. I'd returned to the condo after a period spent at Kim's home, the CEO of the architectural firm where I'd worked for ten years. With Kim, I'd spent all my time inside, in his condo high above the city, or working in the tall tower that housed his company, or enclosed in the tall shadow of his body. Back at my own place, I roamed outside by the river by day, no job to go to, delirious from the sudden change of both scenery and circumstance.

But the feeling that I had to deal with the situation – urgently – had been growing inside me every day. It came to a peak that afternoon. I forced my mind to call up the image of Kim's face, with its remote expression. The phone slid to the floor beside the couch, and the screen went dark, dimming the familiar shapes of the last text exchange between my sister and me, from months back. I shook off the idea that the mere thought of Kim had somehow pushed Amber's words away, down to the floor where I couldn't see them.

I picked the phone up and looked at those words again. The last message she sent me was on March 1st, a month before Kim and I broke up and six months before today: *Are you still living a floating life up there? What do you do up there? I think of you as a god now, living up there in the sky. I bet the wine is good. I think of you when I look up at night. Can you see me? Light a flare from the rooftop if you can, or send a sign – I'm watching. Don't forget.*

I had never answered her, at least not until almost a month later. *Hey*, I'd finally written. *I never responded. I've been kind of floating. Can we talk?* But she never responded.

The year before had been so different. Amber and I saw each other almost every day. We finished each other's spoken and unspoken sentences. Our relationship was symbiotic, each of us sustained by the other on an organic level. One mental picture still came bobbing to the surface of my mind almost every day, even through the fog of that lonely summer – a scene from last September, a hot, summery day. Amber and me, lying on a picnic blanket, the quilt from her bed, spread out on the grass in a park, in a clearing surrounded by trees. A game of Scrabble lay between us, some of the tiles sliding down the board, the game abandoned.

'Here,' she said. 'You can have the rest.' She propped herself up on one elbow and held up a glass bottle of iced tea. She wore a long, shapeless brown sack dress cinched at the waist with a brown leather belt. The outfit combined with the short brown bob that framed her face made her look like a medieval page. Light glinted through the bottle. She looked at me through the gold liquid. 'Now, our important lesson today,' she said. 'Don't think I'm going to forget what we promised. Let's learn how to listen to music again.' I just laughed, not knowing exactly what she meant but also understanding. The sun had started to set. We were both plagued by insomnia, and it was always worse in the summer, so by the fall, we were worn out and jumpy, running on adrenaline and coffee. She pressed a button on her phone and a song started to play, an old song from the 1960s by the Shangri-Las. We both lay back and I closed my eyes.

The sound from the phone was tinny and the lyrics alternately hypnotic and wakening, calling me back, the word 'remember' echoing from a background that was both distant and encompassing. I reached out and paused it, hoping she wouldn't notice. I was getting hungry and too tired. I wondered if I should suggest going to a café. We could sit at a table outside, maybe even buy some cigarettes, even though neither of us had smoked since we were teenagers.

The distant shouts of a soccer game starting up in a field somewhere nearby rose above the trees. I watched a pair of birds – crows – two indistinct black dots against a white cloud, moving in tandem, and it struck me that Amber and I could almost be their shadows on the ground, if we were moving.

Amber and I are fraternal twins, although many people think we look identical. We also have a younger brother, Tom. A bit more than a decade ago, when Amber and I were twenty, I left home to start college. Amber stayed back. She'd left school for a while to take care of Tom, who struggled, unable to go to school himself. As a younger teenager, he'd worked part time at the concession stand of the independent movie theatre where our mom had been the projectionist. But with her gone, he eventually stopped going to that job, too.

While Tom let go of any thoughts of completing his diploma, Amber finished high school by correspondence, working wrapped in blankets from her post on the covered front porch, on the old weather-beaten grey wooden table where Tom would sit beside her and smoke, passing the cigarette to her when she reached out her hand for it. Or sometimes she would be out there alone, even in the rain or the wind. When I would come back home to visit, she would be sitting with her books spread out around her beside the heavy glass ashtray that was always full to overflowing with Tom's butts.

Once released from the claustrophobic halls of high school into teaching herself, Amber had excelled in her studies, earning almost perfect grades in all her courses. She discovered a love of literature, and read voraciously, as though freed: Greek tragedies, the comedies of Neil Simon, the complete works of

Shakespeare, Agatha Christie, H. G. Wells, the Brontës, Robert Louis Stevenson, Arthur Conan Doyle.

We'd grown up less on books than on movies, an interest we got from our mom. She often brought us with her to work when we were kids, and we'd watch whatever she was projecting from above and behind us as we sat side by side in the darkness below, among strangers.

We loved playing in the old brick building that housed the theatre too, while we waited for her to wrap up. The narrow staircase that led to the furnace room was scarred with layers of ancient initials carved into its wooden steps and walls, the furnace itself that hummed below a sleeping robot with many arms. A stack of broken chairs sat behind it on top of some boxes. One day, after managing to pull aside some of the chairs, we opened one of the boxes. In it, we found a small machine that looked like a big, antique camera. We tore the mouldy sides of the box away so we could see it. It was a brown metal box with a brass lens like a squat telescope protruding in the front. There was also a shoebox, which we opened to find a stack of painted glass rectangles with wooden handles. Amber held one up so that the light from the one bulb shone through it. It was a summertime scene of a forest. She held up another one. It was the same scene, but this one autumnal, the trees orange and red. We brought our mom to look, and she kneeled down, holding up the little paintings and running her fingers over the machine.

'It's an old projector,' she said. 'For light shows. They were called magic lanterns. I didn't know this was down here.' She carried the box up with her and put it under the projectionist's desk.

Later, she got some books out of the library and started researching the machine, taking notes in one of her old yellow notepads. I would look through the pictures in some of those books. The images featuring not landscapes but ghosts and ghouls, with their translucent, superimposed quality, were the ones I would stare at, mesmerized.

When we lost her, we all made a shift to reading, not wanting to watch movies as much anymore.

I remember once coming home and finding Tom passed out on the old plaid couch in the living room, Amber sitting beside him in a chair. She was reading to him, and as I listened, I heard that she was reading from *Wuthering Heights* – the scene where Lockwood wakes up to hear a branch knocking against the window. As I walked in, Amber turned to me, and at the same instant Tom opened his eyes.

'Please don't stop reading,' he said.

'It's not a tree,' I said. 'It's something else.'

I thought it would come out sounding playful, but it instead came out in an odd, disconnected tone. It betrayed me, revealing my preference for Amber to come sit on the porch with me, just the two of us, and leave him inside. I went and sat down by his feet. I put them in my lap, as though to say I was sorry. Amber started reading again, with both of us listening.

Tom continued living there, working on the never-ending process of sorting through the house's contents, and never moving out. Amber stayed there with him for periods from time to time so that he wouldn't be alone. I would come to visit, but that was about all I could manage.

I'd been making near daily attempts to get in touch with Amber that spring and summer. By the time I left Kim's condo and come to the place by the river, I was texting and calling her a few times a day with no answer. Last I'd heard, she'd been seeing someone new, a filmmaker, but I wasn't sure if she still was.

As the afternoon started to fade into evening, I was still sitting there, looking out the window, with the phone in my hand, and I decided I would call her again. As I expected, it rang five times and went to voicemail. I let it fall back down to the couch cushion beside me. I was starting to contemplate going back outside when I felt the vibration of an incoming message. I picked it up, my heart racing as I saw that it was from Amber.

It was a group text, not just for me: *Hi folks. I'm here at Glen Iris now. The property is beautiful – bigger than I thought. The movie is coming along well. It's the weddings that are taking up my time but it's worth it if it means we can film here. The house is perfect. It looks as haunted as it feels. Love, AS.*

The house. The wording implied familiarity, as though people reading the message would know what house she meant. Had she written this to people she still talked to, and included my number on the message as an afterthought, thinking of me when I happened to call? Or could she have even added me as a mistake?

That night, as it got dark in my apartment, I opened my laptop and Googled the words *Glen Iris*. The first result was a Facebook account. *Glen Iris Historic House*, a banner on the page said. The profile picture was a painting of a stately brick Victorian mansion with rolling green hills and blue sky behind it. Skimming the page, I gathered that the house was significant because a man named Bertrand Seward, who lived there in the nineteenth century, had been a famous painter in his day. Judging from his work displayed on the page, he had apparently mostly done paintings of his own wealth – his imposing mansion and the large, verdant property it sat on. A slideshow of his paintings of the house and its grounds, intermingled with contemporary photos, slipped by across the screen as I clicked through automatically: slightly impressionistic watercolours of the estate, surrounded at the edge of its lawn by forest; photos showing details of the house's turrets, towers, and porches; and then two images, side by side, captioned 'Available for special bookings!' In one image, formally dressed people surrounded a bride and groom on the lawn, in the other, what looked like a film crew was shooting the house from the front lawn. Amber stood in the middle of the crew, holding a clipboard.

I didn't recognize her right away, but only as the image slipped away to be replaced with a new one, a scene of the house decorated for fall harvest, complete with bales of hay on the porch. I clicked on the screen frantically, trying to pause the slideshow and pull Amber back into view. And there she was again. Her hair had grown out, she was thin, and she was dressed differently, in jeans and a black sweatshirt. She didn't look like herself. But it was definitely her.

I clicked back through more of the pictures and saw her again, in a shot of the mansion. She stood by herself in front of it, smiling. She held a phone in one hand and a pitchfork in the other. Her eyes gleamed as though she'd just been laughing at something the photographer had said, or something she'd said to the photographer. Could she have been making a joke about the American Gothic pose the pitchfork and farmhouse suggested? One of us would have made that joke if I'd been there.

A caption floated below the picture: *Wedding and events coordinator Amber Sledge is here to help you plan your special event.*

The unclear function of the house – was it public or private? a heritage site or an event venue? – coupled with her ambiguous relationship to the place and her changed appearance, disturbed me. I couldn't categorize what she was doing or put it away in my mind. I tried to recall what she'd said about the filmmaker she was seeing, but the few vague fragments she'd told me had grown vaguer as the months had passed. I searched the picture for details as though that might help me understand. I looked more closely at the house itself, and then enlarged the image.

In an upstairs window, I could just make out a grey shape behind the glass. Or maybe it could have been a streak of light, a reflection. But it was in the size and shape of a person's shoulders and head, looking out. I blinked, looked again, and questioned what I thought I'd seen.

In the dark room, my laptop's screen the only light, a bloom of warmth crept up my neck as a thought about Amber formed. While I'd been wrapped up with Kim, I'd assumed I'd been on her mind, that she'd pictured me gazing out the window of his condo into the night sky, thinking of her. I'd never imagined her spending time having her picture taken by someone I didn't know, forgetting me, becoming someone whose life I couldn't imagine.

Kim – my ex-boss and *anti-twin* – had been right, I realized, at least about one thing. It was something he'd once said that I hadn't thought about much at the time. I heard his voice, but this time I really heard what he'd meant, too: 'There's only one way to really see things *fully*, and not just partially,' he'd said one night as we lay together. 'You have to see things mapped on the axes: Y and X. The horizontal relative to the vertical.' Some joke about horizontal positions followed, my effort to end the conversation, which as usual was less interesting to me than the idea of lying there wrapped in each other's limbs, the starry night sky around us out those high, cold windows. But now, suddenly, I recalled it and it clicked.

I saw it laid out before me like a graph illustrating the distance between Amber and me.

He'd drawn me up into the sky. I'd gone so far up the Y axis that I'd lost sight of the ground and where Amber could be found on it. She was a being of the horizontal plane, going out across the world and into it, and I'd just gone up, out of it, away and invisible. It was me who had disappeared, not her. I was the one who had become an idea.

As I began seeing through Kim, I gave him the private nickname of the *anti-twin*. What I'd meant by this at first was that he was my opposite. But over time, I saw that the label was also true in another sense: I emerged from his world, for all intents and purposes, twinless. He had un-twinned me, or at least that's how I felt.

He had other nicknames, some of them dated, from a past life before he'd become the man I met. I knew that he had at one time been a different kind of person, or had at least been understood differently. One of my fellow architectural technicians at Metamorphic had at some point clipped out a magazine article about Kim and posted it in the kitchenette, and I read it over and over while waiting for my coffee to brew: '*The star-seeker*,' it began. 'The imagination of Kim Krol – a star himself in the city he's helping to re-envision – is nothing short of cosmic. As a child, a telescope given to him by his father got him interested in astronomy. In his young adulthood, this turned into an interest in alien life, and how life on Earth might help us to picture other worlds and those worlds' creatures. This is the vision he's brought to the nighttime cityscape.' This was accompanied by a picture of Kim, standing in his twenty-third-floor office beside a telescope on a table, gazing out at a starry night sky: lean, tall, with straight black-and-grey shoulder-length hair. These days, his hair was much more grey than black.

His looks were a topic of some discussion among my co-workers, fuelling a lively ongoing debate over the degree of his appeal. Some found him magnetic. Others, especially those who had met him personally, had the opposite reaction. They were unnerved by the odd, remote look in his eyes behind his glasses, his blank expression, the sense he gave that he wasn't really in the room but somewhere beyond it, already moved on to whatever was next for him in his day.

During my first nine years at Metamorphic, I'd known Kim only from pictures on the company's website and the occasional sighting in a crowded elevator or across the mezzanine. Nonetheless, it was hard for me to imagine Kim spending time as pictured in the magazine article, gazing out and thinking. To me, he always looked so busy, like he was going multiple different places, to multiple different meetings, all at the same time. He seemed to be everywhere and nowhere at once in the building, his presence like a time-lapse video of the paths he walked each day, going from room to room, and floor to floor, a map of criss-crossed streaks of light. He seemed present in the way an atmosphere is, all around. But maybe this feeling was inevitable given the number of hours I spent deep in his designs each day.

Over the years, his aesthetic had incubated in me – this was just part of the job, a necessary part. To design the condos and the company's other products, we had to understand the look that made people desire them – the 'Metamorphic' look.

Metamorphosis was a bridge Kim had designed in 2002. It had won all kinds of prizes and was featured not just in architectural journals but in international mass-market magazines and newspapers. Each day, as I rode the burgundy-upholstered elevator to and from work on the seventh floor, I gazed at the massive, chrome-framed photographs on the elevator walls of aerial nighttime views of the bridge.

There was no denying that the bridge was spectacular. Its diaphanous railings appeared, through a holographic effect of light, to flap like a dragonfly's wings in the night sky, as the lights of cars crawled across its back and were incorporated into the structure's undulating bioluminescence. It was built science-fiction, and it represented the height of his career. The colours of it, the lights, the evocation of some species of gigantic, luminous, alien insect that had landed on the city, were ingrained in me by my daily rides up and down the elevator, not to mention my daily work.

My job was to find new ways of reinterpreting the famous elements of the bridge into reproduceable accents that could be incorporated into condo designs – a wing-like wire-mesh balcony here, a glimmer of shifting alien colour there. These accents were like gift shop miniatures of the original vision.

They stunned and confused the eye like the blinding effect of mirrors refracting bright light. The company had also moved into licencing its brand and images for use in advertisements, so even walking the early-morning or twilit city streets on my way to or from work, the images I'd helped bring forth from Kim's mind were projected around and above me, on signs and electronic billboards in the square near the Metamorphic building. Flicking tails, flickering wings, fragments of life falling through the air. I'd come to feel that I lived inside his mind, that it was a giant cocoon that had expanded to the size of the city, and I was in it, a half-formed thing that never gets born. I wanted to break out, to create my own thing using what I'd learned from Kim's work. It crept up on me, the need to make my mark.

One day, during my lunch break, Amber and I strolled the streets as the season's first snowfall came down around us. I told her I was feeling restless at work. 'I never thought I'd care,' I said. She was quiet that day, and she just listened. 'I mean, I never thought I'd need anything from work. I thought I'd always be happy to just do work at work and find meaning elsewhere. But I want to contribute something. I've been having some ideas about things we could do that we haven't done. With light. We've done lots with metal and paint, but nothing much with light. I've been thinking about stained glass. What we could do with that.'

'What about a magic lantern?'

'*That* creepy old thing,' I said. 'I haven't thought about it in years.'

'Yeah. Except with moving images. Movement might be just what you need.'

I'd been telling her how sedentary I'd been feeling, not just physically but mentally. Spiritually. Like I was being pulled downward. Sometimes by the end of the day I felt like I could hardly walk to the elevator, and yet I couldn't wait to get out into the fresh air.

'I have some notes on the lanterns that Tom gave me recently. Mom's notes that she took when she was interested in them. I can send them to you.'

Back at the office later that day, some pictures arrived in my inbox in an email from Amber. I quickly transcribed the notes into a typed document so no one in the office would see the handwritten document on my screen.

Magic lantern shows, the notes began. *A way of bringing people together. Suspension of disbelief as a group activity. <u>A collective</u> <u>imagining</u>. Of a scene, another landscape. Some were called <u>Dissolving Views</u>. Scenes disappeared and were replaced by new ones. Summer turning into fall, forest into castle, country into city, etc.*

<u>But</u> <u>there</u> <u>was</u> <u>another</u> <u>kind</u>. The dark version of the same thing. A ghost show (phantasmagoria). The phantasmagoria was different. Secretive, ritualistic. Based on disorientation, immersion. People plunged into darkness, sometimes after being made to fast. Or given drugs, wine, electric shocks. Hidden machines projecting ghosts onto smoke.

Magic lantern show: shared. Space re-imagined by agreement. Fantasy as collective vision.

Phantasmagoria: <u>not</u> shared. <u>Not</u> by agreement. A vision imposed. Imagination taken by surprise.

Over the following weeks, I started doing some research of my own, and I learned that there really was a type of show called Dissolving Views, in which one landscape or image would turn into another. More importantly, though, I learned how the mechanics of the machines worked. Stealing time from my other work at my desk, I began drawing up a prototype. I also used AutoCAD to create images for some slides. Scenes of abstract natural imagery dissolved into one another, the colours luminous and rich. The palette was based on Amber's favourites: yellow, green, orange, brown, gold, and red. I thought of my lantern as dedicated to and inspired by her. I wrote a short report about how the lanterns would work, what their effects would be. Their purpose, derived from my mom's notes, would be to turn spaces into shared fantasies.

I cradled my idea, biding my time, thinking over the different ways it and others like it could be installed in the lobbies or exterior spaces to make their walls into moving scenes. Or, alternatively, maybe it could be my own thing, for some use beyond private property, available through a means other than a sale. Maybe it could be a way of moving beyond Metamorphic.

One day, returning to my desk from a lunchtime walk, I was hanging my coat and scarf on a hook on the outside of my cubicle when a voice behind me said my name. I spun around to find Ellis, my manager, standing there.

'I'm wondering if you might have some time to come by my office later this afternoon.'

I stood between her and my computer, looking at her face, trying to read her expression. Glancing back at my computer, I saw that the screen was on and active with two tabs open: one, my email, the other, the drawing of my design for the magic lantern with all its components, instructions, and the images it would project.

I desperately scanned my mind trying to recall whether I'd clicked these windows closed when I left or whether I'd left them open for all to see – evidence that I was doing my own project while I was supposed to be working on a new balcony design.

'I'll call you when I have a moment,' Ellis said, giving me an impassive look before turning and walking briskly to the elevator.

After an anxious afternoon of waiting, I got Ellis's call to go up to her office.

There were printouts of my plans and instructions for the magic lantern laid out in a fanned sheaf on her desk in a manner too precise not to have been by design. The drawings for the slides were open in a file on her computer screen, which was turned to face me.

She gestured for me to sit down across from her. 'Thanks for coming up, Julia,' she said. 'I've been looking at your plans.'

With no time to wonder how long she'd known I was spending company time on a side project at work or to think about the fact that she must have used my computer to forward these files to herself, I answered: 'Yes. It's a lightshow projector.'

'I know,' she said, her tone cryptic. 'Will you walk me through the idea?'

I clicked through the slides, explaining how they would appear and dissolve on the walls of a space. Even just shining from the screen, the images already seemed to glow and change the room around us: a sun shining on orange water appeared, then a wash of yellow light with gold, moth-like shapes flying through it. Then a bird burst out of a dragonfly and disappeared into a scattering of leaf-like shapes. 'The images merge into each other,' I said. I paused, considering my situation. The prospect that I could possibly even be fired. I would have to spin this as an opportunity. Speaking quickly so I didn't have to think about it, I added, 'I was thinking maybe the lanterns could work in our lobbies.'

Ellis dragged one fingernail across the screen where a disembodied insect wing flickered, as though trying to touch it. 'This is very Kim,' she said. She turned around, her face difficult to read. 'This is interesting work. I just wanted us to be on the same page. Okay if I share this with a few people?'

A few weeks later, after several stages of an email thread that I read and reread as plans progressed, unable to focus on my other work, I got an email from Ellis, with Kim copied on it. Our team's new device had made a splash at the opening presentation of a new building, where it had been installed in the lobby. Guests had commented on the atmosphere, how they felt like they were in another world. They apologized that there hadn't been time to invite me – the idea to do a beta run of the lantern at the opening had come up last minute. They'd acknowledged me by name in some remarks at the presentation. Alarm and excitement battled within me, equally matched.

To my utter surprise, a few weeks later, I received a message from Kim's assistant, Ben, inviting me to a pre-holiday lunch with Kim, Ben, and a few members of the executive team.

When I arrived, I found that I was the only one besides Ben who had slogged my way through a terrible, traffic-halting snowstorm to the dark, sleek Italian restaurant at the base of a luxury condo building. Kim sat in a corner, a faint smile on his face. He stood when I approached, and I was struck by how tall he was, but in a somewhat frail rather than strong way. Over an impossibly delicious lunch, featuring olives that tasted like butter instead of salt and roasted tomatoes that seemed to glisten with sun, he led us through a conversation built on questions. Do you enjoy the city? Where else have you lived? Have you spent much time travelling?

Lunch turned into late afternoon drinks, and then we were invited upstairs to the penthouse condo. Kim's home, it turned out. Ben left soon, and Kim and I spent the night talking. He was soft-spoken. He would have been a good conversationalist if it weren't for his seeming compulsion to ask me questions, as though someone had told him he should and he'd memorized the rule.

I was invited for dinner another night that week. And then more evenings in the weeks following. I slept there one night, and he slept on the couch. I slept there again, and this time, he didn't. It wasn't complicated. The trip up and down the elevator of his building became part of my daily commute. Kim had a small but striking collection of plants. He was interested in rare species and mentioned something once about research into breeding bioluminescent flora. One of his plants was a large, spiky bromeliad with sea-creaturish scales. Another, a large, white, stone-like succulent – *pseudolithos migiurtinus* – almost glowed within a dish of the rocks it so resembled. 'Biomimicry is an untapped power,' Kim said, as I looked at it. In the cool, silent, un-living space, the aliveness of the plants seemed to hum. I felt entranced by their presence when I was there, like I was tuning into them and out of the human realm.

Before long, I began spending all my time at Kim's penthouse. It wasn't something I could ever have predicted, and it isn't a choice I can explain. I left my apartment empty. I didn't even think about the rent I continued paying for an empty place.

What I loved about that period most of all was how much space Kim gave me. I would sit in his condo when he was out at work or travelling or working in another room. The unit occupied the entire top floor and as much as I wanted not to, I loved it. I loved the feeling of being so high up, so remote. It was like a drug, the pills Tom used to give me sometimes when we were teenagers that we said felt like a blanket wrapped around the cold part of our brains. From my spot on a long, white couch in the centre of the living space, in front of the panoramic windows that curved all the way around the circular building, I would gaze out at the view, feeling the plants' company. By day, in the winter light, snow falling lightly outside, the apartment was like a jewel box – ornaments, trinkets, antiquities, oddities, relics, and pieces of art sat on all manner of carved wooden shelves, tables, and chests. By night, sitting in the dark, looking out, the place felt astral, like a slice of captured space, a flying saucer invisible against the sky where it hovered.

Our connection wasn't especially physical once we settled into a pattern, although we did sleep in the same bed. I never told him this, of course, but when the lights were out and we were lying there, I didn't feel like I was lying beside a man. Instead, aware of his long, delicate bones on the mattress beside me, I felt that I was next to the frame of a large, long bird, an ibis maybe, or a crane, who had flown up through the sky and through the window by night. Sometimes I would see that he wasn't sleeping. That he was lying there with his eyes open, looking not toward the window but straight up at the ceiling. Though he was hard to read, he was easy to be around, more like a vapour than a person.

about Tom too, about how long it had been since any of us had seen each other.

She crossed her arms, looking nervous, almost formal. I didn't want to see her like that, but I also wanted to try to address how things seemed to have shifted, not just that night but in general.

'Amber,' I said. 'I'm sorry we've lost touch.'

'It's not your fault,' she said. 'It's just the way things are. Things have been busy for me too. It's been hard to see people – to make plans. But now that we're together, I feel like we're back on track.'

She stood up and carried our glasses to the kitchen. I followed her, not wanting to lose hold of the conversation. In the kitchen, the hundred-dollar bills and the note still lay on the counter. I crumpled them in my palm and stuffed them in my pocket. The suggestion of a transaction between me and Kim – him buying his way out of being there and not even hiding effectively – wasn't something I wanted Amber to perceive. I hoped she hadn't noticed the money.

'I feel weird asking … but Tom wanted to know if he could borrow some money. I've lent him as much as I can afford this month. I might stop in to see him on my way home, and if you wanted to, I could bring him something from you. Only if you wanted.'

I pulled the bills out of my pocket and pressed them into her hand. After the door was closed behind her, I realized we hadn't hugged goodbye as we normally did.

When Kim got in, it was after one. I pretended to be half asleep as he got into bed beside me.

'Did you have a nice night with your sister?' he asked.

'It was perfect.'

'Because I wasn't there?'

'Because she was here. It was exactly what I needed.'

'I'm glad,' he said, wrapping his arms around me and pulling me close. As he drew me in, I closed my eyes. In the back of my mind, I knew Kim had made an excuse to avoid meeting Amber – that he hadn't even tried very hard. He'd only gone down to the restaurant. And yet it was okay. We were floating, in the same larger space, but in our own orbits.

A familiar, easy remoteness settled into my mind, with an effect like conversation overheard from another room: the feeling that people are near and even though you don't have to talk to them or get up for anything, they're still a kind of company.

The next evening, Kim and I were both in the kitchen, each getting our own drinks and food, when I was somehow struck by the thought that if I were to disappear into thin air in front of him, that moment, he would raise an eyebrow, but then turn around, humming, and put water on for tea, comforted by routine domestic pleasures, the haze of his daily motions.

A few weeks later, at my own place, where I'd gone to pick up some mail while Kim was away on a trip, my phone rang. I expected it to be Kim, but Ben's name came up on the screen. I was startled by the clipped, formal tone of his greeting.

'Look, Julia. I'm sorry to have to break some news to you. It might come as a bit of a surprise, but then again, maybe it won't. Ellis has been reviewing some company emails and other records of your work and found that you've been redirecting some company time.'

'But I was designing the lanterns,' I said.

'Julia, we really appreciate your work, but we really feel that you seem interested in exploring other projects, and we see that as a positive thing. We want to let you go do that. You have lots going for you, and lots of talent. There are other exciting things out there for you. And we're offering you a generous severance package. We want to make it fair. I'll email it to you today.'

Then, four hours later, when I read the details of the severance, I saw, with rage ringing in my ears, that Kim owned all my designs, including the projectors and the images used in them. I drafted and sent an email to Kim, my final word to him, my own form of severance. I called a lawyer, someone I knew from school, but there wasn't much I could do without spending a fortune.

Not that I had much time to think about the loss of the lanterns. I was too busy thinking about the word 'severance,' a word I was grateful for because of the finality it gave my break with Kim and what he had brought out in me. I was also busy on the calculator on my phone, dividing a lump sum by the number of days it covered.

After a few days back at my place, a new worry arose: I learned that the owner of the building had put the place up for sale, and one by one each tenant had moved out. The only renters left were me and the guys upstairs, who told me they were going to ride it out until the landlord escorted them off the property, if it came to that. I'd missed all the landlord's notices telling me to move out while I was at Kim's. I read through them. I had until the end of September before I had to go.

As I sat by the river, trying to figure out what I should do next, I realized that over the course of my relationship with Kim and its complicated ending, I'd lost touch with everyone in my life, including Amber. The severance from my job was just a shadow: the real rupture was from my sister.

Three days after I got Amber's text message about Glen Iris, an unexpected visitor appeared at my building. It was on a rainy afternoon as I got home from some errands and entered the building's foyer. I'd gotten caught without an umbrella. As I faced outside while shaking rain from my light jacket, I realized, even before I began to turn to face the interior of the building, that someone was standing there behind me, in the stairwell leading up to my apartment; mine was the only apartment in that wing that seemed to be occupied, so whoever it was must be there to see me.

As I turned, my mind raced through the short list of people who could possibly be standing there, with bursts of fear, anger, and joy mingling as I imagined it could be the landlord, Kim, Amber.

It was Tom. His brown hair had grown out, and his eyes were clear behind his glasses. Even after all the time that had passed, the instant glance to check his eyes was still a reflex – they were his mood rings, we used to say. He was wearing a red sweater, and the colour made him look more solid and healthy than I'd seen him in years, either in my mind or in person. He was more *tangible* somehow.

'Julia,' he said, taking one step down the stairs toward me. 'I'm sorry to show up like this without telling you.'

'Tom!' I said. I would have cried if I hadn't been so surprised. We met on the bottom stair and I threw my arms around him, showering his red sweater with raindrops. 'I've missed you so much.' I stood back and looked at him.

'You're all wet,' he said, wiping some of the rain off my shoulder.

He was still thin but looked strong. The sweater was soft and looked expensive. I'd never seen him dressed this way. In my mind he still wore the long-sleeved metal-band shirts, the fabric stretched tight over his forearms.

There had always been something ethereal about Tom; in the past, he was so often lying down, or sitting, or sleeping, while others were standing or walking. Sometimes you'd think he'd heard something you said, and then he wouldn't remember a thing about it. Other times, he would tell you things you didn't recall ever telling him, that you thought only you knew, summed up with emotional precision and complete under-standing. He had also had a way of disappearing, or, conversely, of being there when you didn't think he was. But that was then. Now, he just looked focused. And good. He was standing there looking right at me. It was nice to see him like that, and yet also disconcerting, a reminder of how much time had gone by – and also, maybe, an indicator that I'd gotten him wrong. He looked like he was doing better than I was.

'Well, I'm glad to hear that,' he said. 'I was nervous about coming. I wasn't sure if you'd want to see me or not. It's been such a long time. I've missed you. And Amber.'

'Why weren't you sure if I'd want to see you? Why would you ever question that?'

'I don't know. I just stopped hearing from either of you, so I didn't know what to think. I think Amber's mad at me or something. She was staying with me at the house for a while. She helped me sort through some of Mom's things, and that was nice. But then things shifted and she started spending most of her time with this guy, Orin. She said he's nice, but I'm not sure. He's a filmmaker and was getting her to do all kinds of things to help out with his work on a movie. She said he was going to pay her when the film was made. It's some kind of ghost story, apparently, which only makes the whole situation weirder. She's living at the house where they're filming. It's a historic mansion out in the middle of nowhere. But they're also running events, running an Airbnb – all the things the family who owns the house does to make money from the house until they have time to sell it. It sounds pretty crazy. Did you get her text?'

'Yes,' I said. 'I'm so worried. I feel like things aren't okay.'

'No,' he said. 'I don't think they are. She's changed. I'm starting to feel pretty worried. Why isn't she in touch with me? Or you? If you're not busy, maybe I can come up and talk?'

In my apartment, I went to go change into something dry. When I came back, I saw that Tom had found some vodka and a bottle of tonic in the fridge and was making a drink. I thought about asking him if that was a good idea but then felt unable to say it, not wanting to make assumptions after being apart for so long.

'I don't drink much anymore,' he said, clearly aware of my thoughts. 'This afternoon is just to celebrate seeing you again. Well, maybe *celebration* isn't the right word – it's something closer to relief, like when you thought something might be over but then you find out it doesn't have to be. Actually, this year has been a time of finding out that things don't have to be so bad. Or at least not as bad as I thought they had to be.' He told me he had been taking some medication that had helped him.

We sat on the couch. His voice grew blurrier as he made more drinks, though it was early in the afternoon. I watched him, sitting at the opposite end of the couch. He began to sink down into the cushions, hair growing unkempt, eyes darkening and dulling. I had a drink too, trying to allay my anxiety. The level in the vodka bottle was dropping. Tom was looking more and more like the old, unfocused Tom, and we still hadn't even begun talking about Amber or what we should do next.

I looked at the clock. It was half past three. I glanced outside. The sun had come out, shining bright and golden, but one long grey cloud moved across the sky beside it.

'Look, Tom. We have to figure out what to do about Amber.'

'I know.'

'I just don't know what's happened to her. She looks so different now. Look.' I unlocked my phone to show him an old photo. 'Look at her a few years back.'

He took the phone from me and studied the photo, his expression pensive.

The picture was the Amber I remembered, her platonic form, the Amber who lived in a deep place in my mind: her short brown bob framing her face like a flower, an open expression in her eyes, and a self-possessed stance. The similarity between us was strongest in our eyes: they were the same shape, and we shared the same too-frank gaze.

'And look now,' I said, opening a second picture, the one from the Glen Iris House website, holding it up for him to see. The ripped jeans, the long, unkempt hair, the sweatshirt. In this picture you could see how thin she was. Her jaw looked tight, and she looked tired. She had dark circles under her eyes.

'Oh.'

'You see what I mean?'

'I do.'

'She's different.'

'She is.' He pushed his chair out, stood and got his wallet and keys from where they had fallen on the floor earlier.

'Well,' he said. 'It's a good thing I have a car here. We can get going now if you're ready. And if you don't mind driving. Too bad the sun didn't stay around. Looks like rain again.' I looked out the window and saw the darkening sky, and then looked at him, seeing a similar cloudiness in his eyes.

I got my keys, a sweater, and an umbrella, and we locked up and left. Though going to look for Amber at the house was the right thing to do, it didn't exactly feel that way. In fact, I felt a sense of unease that only grew stronger as we got nearer to it.

It rained the whole way. I was surprised by how hilly it became, how forested, even though we were still close to the city, just thirty minutes from downtown. Still, as we drove, the minutes seemed like hours, and the hills hid what lay beyond them. I worried about how Amber would react when she saw us. I caught myself gripping the wheel too tightly, my shoulders hunched and hands clenched. With great effort, I willed my fingers to loosen and my shoulders to relax. As we arrived at Glen Iris House, the rain let up and the sun came out in a corner of the sky. We pulled into a gravel parking lot along one side of the property, parked, and got out of the car.

I'd been so caught up with uneasiness and worry that I'd forgotten how novel it was to get out of the city. The light was golden in the sky above us. Ahead, the landscape rose into green hills to our left, and to the right, it dipped down into misted valleys. Wildflowers swayed in the breeze – tiger lilies, Queen Anne's lace, and echinacea. Tall trees rose around the house in a ring. The smell was crisp, and a few brightly coloured leaves twirled down through the air.

And then there was the house itself, which I'd seen in the pictures online. It rose tall before us, its towers and turrets making it look like something you would expect to find in a Carpathian foothill rather than so close to the city. And for all its resplendence, it was a touch derelict, with a broken shutter here, a rotten section of porch there. And one window in a high tower that was broken and patched with what looked like thick silver tape. But it was gorgeous, almost beyond belief, mostly because of the natural surroundings. It was sheltered on all sides by cedars, spruces, and maples, and in the gaps between them, rolling hills could be seen in the distance. The vegetation was in full late-summer decadence, everything swaying and buzzing, blazing with colour. Shifting light and shadows washed the dripping, rustling leaves in slanting sunbeams.

We stood there in front of the house. It was a strange moment. How do you approach a building when you're not sure exactly what it is? I couldn't imagine us having to approach it and step up on its old wooden porch with its trellised sides, as though it were a home, as if we were visiting someone who'd invited us. But then, almost as though we were expected, a woman walked out onto the porch and stepped forward, her hand up to shade her eyes, looking at us.

I felt like I was arriving home, not to a place but to a person.

It was my sister, with her new, longer hair. I ran toward her and threw my arms around her, holding her shoulders and stepping back to study her face.

'Julia,' she said, smiling. Surprise and relief mingled in her eyes. 'Thank god you're here. It's been so long.'

'I've been trying to reach you. It's been way too long – I don't know how or why, but we can't let it happen again.'

'It's been a strange time for me. Stranger than I can even tell you.' She looked at me as if that should be enough. I didn't know what to say. It had been strange for me too. How could we begin to understand one another again, especially there in that odd place?

For the moment, routine came to the rescue. Amber glanced back into the house and laughed.

'It's just been so busy,' she said, speaking more quickly than the old Amber would have. 'It's been hard to even think. Every day, it just gets busier. Tonight's our first fall wedding, and that's a huge deal for us. It's all I've been doing, getting ready for it. All I want is to sit down with you and talk. But in a couple of hours, two hundred people are going to arrive for a party behind the house.'

Tom stepped out from behind me, and it was as though Amber had seen only me up until then.

'Tom!' she said. He ran up to her and she clasped him in her arms. 'Well, let's use the time we have to talk. Come into the house. We can sit down. Together.'

We stepped through the front door and found ourselves in an oak-panelled hall. She led us through it into a sitting room in which almost everything visible was made of wood: the floors and the furniture, which was spare – just a table and some chairs, and a rocking chair in a corner beside a stone fireplace. The windows were yellowed and wavy with age. The only decoration was a row of milk-glass vases on the windowsill.

Amber led us to the kitchen at the back of the house, and we gathered around a table.

'Sit down,' she said. 'There's so much to say and we'll have to find time for it all. I hope you'll stay here tonight. Please do. I could really use the company. I mean, company I know. Besides Orin. There will be lots of company I don't know. To be honest, I'm feeling in over my head.'

'Stay where?'

'Here. In the house. The family who owns it rents it out through Airbnb in the summer and the rooms are still set up. We take down the sets when people come, or close doors to hide them. No occupancies tonight, thank goodness, aside from me and Orin. The wedding guests are staying at a hotel in the next town.'

'Amber, are you living here? I mean, is this home for you now?'

'I don't really *live* anywhere these days, exactly. I've been staying here, I guess. Working here. Being here. All I do is work.'

'What do you do here?'

'A bit of everything. I only came here to work on Orin's film, but the house's owners have us helping out with hosting events in exchange for letting us film here. We've become kind of like caretakers. Weddings are their big thing in the summer. Tonight's is a big one. It's a harvest theme.'

'What's your role in it?'

'The scope of my role has kind of crept beyond the original idea. I started off as a kind of host or facilitator for the wedding, and now I'm something closer to an artistic director. I've been preparing for days. They couldn't decide on the theme, exactly. One of them wanted a harvest theme, and the other wanted an eco theme. The motif of the decorations is moons and dragonflies. I'm filming the whole thing.' She lowered her voice and continued. 'The couple wants me to film the night as a wedding video. Orin wants me to film it at the same time in another way, secretly. So we can use it as a scene in his film. He has some crazy plans for this evening. I don't know yet what I'm going to do. The truth is, I think I'm going to leave, but Orin isn't going to be happy about it, so I wanted to wait until we got through this wedding, at least.'

'You could always come back with us.'

'Maybe. But first, I have to get through tonight. At least you guys are here.' She glanced around the room for a moment, as if trying to locate something. 'Hey, why don't we have a drink? Actually, I already decided that I'm going to have a drink tonight, whether I'm technically on the job or not.'

She stood up and walked over to a low cupboard at the back of the kitchen. Inside were rows of red wine, whiskey, vodka, and gin. She chose a bottle of red and unscrewed it.

'Tom, do you want water? Or is a bit of wine okay?'

'I think a bit of wine is okay for today,' he said. 'I could use it.'

'Those bottles are for the wedding, but there's way more than we'll need.' She poured us each a generous amount.

In a kind of awkward half-joke, we clinked our glasses. The sound was too loud in the quiet house, and the gesture felt almost staged after not being together for so long. For one strange moment, I thought about leaving, just getting up and going, and grabbing Amber as I did, pulling her with me, like she was a paper doll that could be moved from scene to scene at will.

'Tell me how you are,' Amber said. She was looking at me, not Tom.

I told her how things had ended with Kim. About how much I'd missed her and regretted losing touch. It all came out in a rush, and before I realized, I'd been going on too much, almost like I was pleading. I stopped myself. I reached my hands out toward her on the table.

'How are you, though?'

'I'm okay,' she said. 'I'll have to explain everything. But I hope you know I miss you and love you. I thought you'd found … something else, and then I met Orin. He's helped me a lot, he really has.' She crossed her arms over her chest and closed her eyes for a second, as though trying to clear her mind. 'But now I have this awful feeling that I can't get out of it. Even though I know I can. Whenever I want. There's nothing stopping me from leaving. But I can't shake the feeling that I can't. The house scares me but it also feels hard to leave. A farmer I met in the next town told me there's asbestos in the walls. And yet I haven't found time to plan to get away.'

'You can stay with me,' I said. As I spoke the words, I realized I would have to leave my place soon. But we would figure something out. As long as we were together, we could go anywhere.

'I'd like that,' she said. 'I'll do that. If I come back.'

Tom poured us all another glass of wine, finishing off the bottle. He walked to the cupboard and opened it, turning around to look at Amber. She nodded, and he brought another bottle to the table.

'They're going to be here soon,' Amber said. 'Do you want to go outside and see my creation before everyone shows up? I'm sick of the whole thing, but still, it was a lot of work. I'm proud of it. Despite the circumstances.'

She walked over to a door that led from the kitchen to the back of the house, and we followed her out onto a porch. It was starting to get dark. The back lawn was set up with tables and chairs. Around the perimeter, screens of diaphanous fabric hung from threads to form four semi-transparent walls that shimmered in the dusky light. We stepped down from the porch and walked into the area enclosed by the screens.

'Come,' Amber said, gesturing for us to follow her to the middle of the space. 'I'll show you.' As we walked with her across the lawn, I saw it, sitting on a table: the magic lantern from the theatre. I hadn't seen it in years. We sat down. It was getting darker. She turned on the machine, and as it whirred to life, beams of rich incandescent light streamed out of the lenses. Thousands of painted dragonflies appeared on the fabric screens interspersed with little orange harvest moons and tiny gold stars.

'You made new slides for it,' said Tom.

'My phantasmagoria,' she said. 'I've come to think of it as a kind of ghost show. Because there are no actual dragonflies here. Not that I've seen.'

She laughed. Once, when we were kids and shared a room, our window finally broke where there'd been a crack for years. Amber bumped up against it and it just shattered. When we realized what she'd done, we pulled out this old rose-patterned blanket and a stepladder and hung the blanket over the window. But once it was up, we both just stood there. We'd thought it might look nice, but the wind sucked the fabric up into the broken pane, pressing it against the glass, and the light revealed the shabby, bare threads of the blanket. It looked old, mottled and stained. And when it breathed in and out with the wind, it was a monstrosity. We started crying and ran downstairs to tell our mom what we'd done.

From behind us, I heard a cough. I turned. A man was stepping toward us through the tables. He was wearing a suit.

'Orin,' Amber said, standing.

He walked up to us, smiling.

'Congratulations,' he said, his arm outstretched to shake our hands. We stood, too confused to know what to say to his congratulations. Tom shook hands first, and then it was my turn. As I shook his hand and looked into his eyes, I could tell from his comment and his smile that he thought we were the couple getting married there that night.

'You must be very excited,' he said.

'No, no, Orin,' Amber said. 'This isn't the couple. This is my brother and sister. Julia and Tom. They're going to stay here tonight. If that's okay.'

His face changed. Was it a look of unease or something else? Then he composed himself and laughed.

'Oh, my mistake. It's nice to meet you – and good to have you here. Amber's told me so much about you. It's going to be a great night. These setups always seem a bit contrived at first, but once the people are here, together, everything comes to life. And Amber's done such a beautiful job. So that I can keep working on my baby.' He laughed again, as if he were embarrassed or sensed that he should seem to be.

'It's due any day now,' Amber said. 'He forgets that you might have come here to see me, rather than for anything to do with our projects.'

He seemed to ignore this comment, and I wasn't sure if he picked up on the tone I'd perceived immediately. If so, he didn't show it. He sat down with us at the table, next to Amber. He put his arm around her shoulder.

I was staring intently at a banner that hung across the back panel of fabric: a slogan was written on it in glittery, coloured letters. *Brightness falls from the air.*

'Maybe next time, it'll be us doing the fun part and not the planning part,' he said, winking. I sneaked a look at Amber. Her eyes widened, and she looked down.

'I mean maybe if we ever want to get married, we could do it here. Who knows, maybe this could be home and not just work. Imagine it. The family who owns it all live abroad now. They just want someone to take care of it, make sure the house generates at least some income. We could make a pitch to be the caretakers in exchange for staying here. Maybe it's not technically a home anymore, but it's still a house and we could make it a home. You guys would be free to visit whenever you want, of course. Or even come stay here. Join us. I know how close you all were growing up.'

'It's a set,' Amber said in an abstracted way, staring past Orin into the darkness visible through a space between two of the screens. 'For a ghost story. We play the ghosts.'

'Speaking of which,' Orin said to Amber. 'Do you have our little show all ready?'

'Yes,' Amber said. 'The ghost is in the machine.' She turned to me. 'Orin asked me to make a special slide for later tonight. The wedding might have an unexpected guest.'

'Amber did such a good job,' Orin said, his eyes gleaming. 'The ghost is actually terrifying. It's amazing what those Victorians and their magic lanterns could manage in terms of special effects, using only some paint and light. A lot more compelling than a lot of the CGI we see now. And scarier. Amber modelled it on an old painting of a ghost but updated it. You should see the way it floats.' He clasped his hands together and looked at Amber. She turned to me, giving me a look I understood right away: she wanted to get out of there.

'Remember, Amber,' Orin said. 'Once everyone's been drinking and things are getting messy. As we know they will, inevitably. Bring up the slide.'

'You know this might cost us the house. Our relationship with the family who owns this place,' Amber said to Orin. 'Or we could even get sued. You'll never be able to use it in the movie.'

'Nah. They'll think it's fun,' he said. 'Or we can say it was an accident. That you put in the wrong slide unintentionally. They'll be having fun. They won't even remember it. And who doesn't want to be in a movie? Besides, if things don't work out, we can always blame it on the harvest moon ... '

I looked at Tom. What was he thinking? He was slumped down in his chair, his cheeks flushed, eyes unfocused. The bottle of wine in front of him was almost empty. I didn't realize he'd brought it out. He picked up his glass and drank the last sip.

'Let's stay,' he said, turning to me. 'Let's go to the wedding. It'd be nice to spend some time together, have some drinks. It'll be fun. We can all be together.' I didn't think he'd been following the stuff about the ghost slide. He looked too out of it.

'That's the spirit,' Orin said. 'Actually, the couple mentioned in an email that they were worried about attendance because of the rain. I bet they wouldn't mind some extra guests.'

It was almost dark now. The contrast between the light on the bright fabric and the dark woods beyond had turned the fabric walls more distinct, almost opaque. The dragonflies, moons, and stars appeared to shimmer and move as the fabric swayed in the breeze.

'Well, hello! Welcome! And congratulations!' Orin stood up and walked toward a couple in a white dress and black tuxedo who were peeking nervously from behind a curtain. Amber stood up and followed, smiling and reaching out her hands to greet them.

Tom and I didn't end up staying at the wedding long. Instead, I helped him into bed about an hour later, as the guests were drinking and dancing. As we left, Amber and Orin were dancing, each with one of the guests.

The bedrooms on the second floor were old, oak-panelled, and austere with high ceilings and tall, dark windows, but the bedding was as bright and clean as you'd expect in a hotel, with matching towels set in neat little stacks on the turned-down sheets.

I lay in bed and listened to the sounds from the party below. Music was playing above a hum of voices. I thought, everyone must be dancing now. Laughter rose up in bursts, and I imagined it breaking over the crowd like tiny fireworks before raining down again. I felt my body relax, despite my unease being in the house. The thought of the asbestos. The night-fracturing moment of a scream and cries from the crowd that I thought must be coming at any moment when the ghost appeared.

A scream never came. Or maybe by the time it did, I was already asleep.

I let go of my thoughts and sank into the warmth of the bed, comforted by the sound of Amber's laugh, even if I couldn't be totally sure if it was her or just someone who sounded like her.

Parametrics of Purity

Jean Marc Ah-Sen

For George Mantzios and Behzad Molavi.

The Translassic Society was the name writers and musicians Artepo Lepoitevin, Kilworthy Tanner, Jean Marc Ah-Sen, Bedegraine Boisrond, Sullivan Strobl, Carlos Reppion, Sasithorn Boontueanthab, Lovel Focillion, and Elpenor Khalid-Morein were billed under in their summer 2007 travels across the tristate area of the United States and select eastern cities of Canada. The fifteen-city reading tour ended in financial disaster, the informal collective dissolving almost as soon as it had been formed due to a clash of personalities. A limited-edition tour program entitled The Thumperous Translassitude Reading Road Pilgrimage *contained written contributions from all of the participants and was offered for purchase at every stop of the tour. A highly-sought-after artifact due to its relatively small print run, the following selection from the program was authored by Ah-Sen.*

A fictional chronicle of how the members of the Society came to work together, 'Parametrics of Purity' was written in the manner of a faux–correspondence writing course and incorporated elements of Lepoitevin's real rise to fame as a tribute to the self-styled impresario who helped finance and underwrite significant portions of the tour's expenses.

꽃

Translassic Meridians and Binomials

What is Translassitude? What is its relation to paralassitude, omnilassitude, and hyperlassitude?

To answer these questions, I must posit an antecedent root and discuss the life and writing of Kilworthy Tanner, my erstwhile writing partner, lover, and confidante. It was Kilworthy and I who brought these terms into current usage – and with the exactitude that has come to characterize all of our writings. One simply does not arrive at 'Translassitude' so much as become a resignifying representation – a concatenating loop – of its principle mechanics and methodology, after having undergone the transfiguring states of being known as para-, omni-, and hyperlassitude, respectively.

I will forego the handwaving I am known for by putting forth a working definition of Translassitude, as the movement I have come to embody has suffered no shortage of dabblers and ex-Translassists contributing ambiguity to its history. I will additionally have relieved myself of the burden of clearing away misconceptions of this burgeoning literary principle, which boasts hundreds of new adherents with each passing year.

Translassitude is the literary science of fictive movement by fictive inaction. Lassitude must not be confused with inertia; movement contradicted by itself is a lost cause of the rudest order. The question is one of circumference, circumvention – in short, of circumlassitude, of meridians and binomials, not of static points and places. Translassitude is a transfinite philosophy of the highest poetic order, and can contain within its extraordinary compass purposeful writing arising from a vast array of protoliterary and protoprosaic motives. Any writer wishing to be in the best standing should possess an awareness of the expedients and dodges from the Translassic arsenal.

I will first relate a few points about its early origins as a response to another system of literary application (lately fallen into disrepute) before going into further detail about Translassitude's truly Daedalean particulars.

Artepoist/Sudimentarist

Artepoism, also known by its more popular cognate Sudimentarism, was a hypno-realist paradise that could not progress beyond the crawling stage of development. It was promulgated exclusively by Artepo Lepoitevin, the primitivist miniature painter who exported the hypno-realist movement's ideas into non-sculptural forms; he was known mostly for being aggressively suicidal. His novel *Artepoist* was published in the mid-seventies when such literary extroversions were tolerated and in some domains even held up as an ill-judged final frontier of what was possible in literature. It is considered the first serious work composed in the Sudimentarist style, consolidating into practice what would become its chief tenets and aesthetic boundaries.

Its most prominent feature was what could only be described considerately as an obsession with the silent tempo of life, stolen moments of calm, inactivity, and boredom reigning unchecked in the obscurity of seclusion; it was the artistic equivalent of a block of concrete drying. This was reflected at the prose level: narrative as lull and hebetude. It made for torturous reading. However, so Sudimentarists (and by extension the hypno-realists) argued, the banausic rhythms of the mundane world would make the rare moments of tensity more bountiful – stalwart and valorous, Sudimentar-like.

Selworthy Sudimentar, the voice that narrates *Artepoist*, attempts to beatify placidity in life in every way possible; but his attitude toward death, the ultimate articulation of repose, remains incongruously hostile (and the striking opposite of Lepoitevin's longing for a quietus ever out of reach). Death is not the end of mankind's suffering; for Sudimentar, it is the insult from which recovery is impossible, a derogation of humanity and a matter of denuding inevitability. The only apparent solutions before Sudimentar are (1) silent surrender to the thermodynamic principle, or (2) a grubby attempt at cultural immortality through the arts. Neither option is deemed acceptable.

The result of this impasse is that Sudimentar makes a deft transition into Artepoism in the same way that Artepo Lepoitevin makes a parallel transition into Sudimentarism: they become mythological emissaries of an imaginary other, fictional counterparts borrowing from a repertory of mostly invented abjections and triumphs with the intention of escaping time's incontestable dominion over being.

Hypno-Reality

Artepo believed he had discovered the ultimate hypno-realist expression of *stillness* in his attempts to live the life of a man he invented – he theorized that there was no greater quietude than boredom that sprang from familiarity, the familiarity of adopting a role and acting commensurately with that office. To its awesome credit, this familiarity also removed a sheen of morbidity around the assumptive calculation of Sudimentar's death, solving Lepoitevin's so-called need for an expedited demise: suicide began to take on a pedestrian colouring. He finally realized that his dark thoughts did not originate in feelings of despair, but were the dregs of a contrarian nature resisting the orthodoxy of hypno-realist principles. The longing for the void abandoned him once he had mastered hypno-reality by enacting Sudimentarism, the *froideur* between life and death having vanished in a puff of ipseity.

For the character of Sudimentar, assuming the 'fictional' role of Artepo Lepoitevin enabled him to dodge assaults from the strong throwing arm of reality (what else is chimerical living good for?), staving off in the process a cognitive blow to his sanity that presumed he had to die like all of mankind. It was a nimble piece of sophistry that allowed him to believe that his own passing would only be the destruction of the Lepoitevin simulacrum, the 'achievement of nonbeing' not unlike dismantling a rather inconsequential piece of furniture.

The fact that this great solution turned on the principle of mimicry with an idealization – and not just any old exemplar, but one that was essentially borne from one's own intellectual mass – put Artepo at odds with the hypno-realist school, which rejected any notion that did not cow to a fanatical, at times overweening positivism. Lepoitevin could not abandon Sudimentarism because it solved his need for annihilation through a kind of *participation mystique*: Artepo would inherit Selworthy's fixation with prolonging hypno-realist pacificity into immortality, exceeding his own desire to kill himself, in the exact degree that Sudimentar would adopt the entire Lepoitevin persona and with it, Artepo's emotional inhibitions and complexes.

Annular Stillness

The one gruelling task left for Artepo was to pencil in the nature of Sudimentar's death at the end of *Artepoist* and render it in such a palatable fashion that he could trot to this rendezvous with a pale horse bearing something resembling a disinterested air, and the furthest thing from a demented gusto. A suicide pact with a lover was the most he could muster: Lepoitevin could then delay the creditable deed until he found someone who could satisfy his fastidious requirements in a consort (his wife had died from an inoperable brain tumour). One presumes Selworthy's twin assumption of his creator's identity was merely a narrative formality needed to close Artepo's circuit of symmetry – another hypno-realist component he could not shake ('annular stillness is eternal stillness,' so the credo went).

Artepo could not resist the allure of the movement he was giving birth to, and at this point abandoned his hypno-realist affiliation; the boost to his credentials that might follow Sudimentarism taking root in the popular consciousness of the masses proved far too alluring (in any event, he might sell more paintings). The popular appetite of the period for new spiritualisms that merged the divinity of the self with an autocratic asceticism practically assured Artepoism's overnight success in certain literary circles, especially those that wanted to lend a deterministic vein to affirmations of the mind.

Khalid-Moreinism

A discussion of the narrative particulars in *Artepoist* will benefit us by bringing the subject of Sudimentarism's paltry relevance to Translassitude to a close.

The ending of *Artepoist* is hotly contested, and some doubt is cast on the viability of Sudimentar's pseudo-rational endeavours – this is complicated by the fact that Lepoitevin refuses to publicly address the book on an interpretive level to non-Sudimentarists.

The mythomane Sudimentar develops a small following of pursuivants in need of an authority figure to give direction to their lives. Sudimentar encourages them to compose works of literature in the Artepoist style and to assume the identities of their main protagonists; naturally, to promote and maintain praxeological conformity to these opuscules proves a touch more difficult.

One of Sudimentar's followers, a man named Elpenor Khalid-Morein, composes a revealing portrait of the Artepoist commune and its eponymous leader in an exegetical text of his own called *Khalid-Moreinism*. In a move of startling heterodoxy, the fictional character he hopes to incorporate into his life is that of Selworthy Sudimentar himself. Elpenor writes about the infinite-regress problem in Sudimentar's novel-within-a-novel *Sudimentarist*, which involves Artepo Lepoitevin, a primitivist painter who is writing a book about Sudimentarism called *Artepoist*.

Khalid-Morein finds two major faults with *Sudimentarist*, which he voices without reservation in the hope of making Artepoism stronger from within. The vicious paradox entailed by *Sudimentarist* should presume a high degree of self-awareness on the part of the Artepo Lepoitevin 'character,' who must be intimately familiar with Sudimentar's own attempts to write a fictional account of Artepoism. The fact that the Lepoitevin character in *Sudimentarist* displays no outward signs of this awareness is a logical error.

The second failure of the novel concerns the *fourberie* of wanting to switch places with Lepoitevin while Lepoitevin wants to assume Sudimentar's identity: there is no actual reversal occurring – only the treachery of interpolation exists. A war on death is a doomed war on time, inasmuch as the man of the future cannot be constitutionally dissimilar from the man of the past. Sudimentar and Lepoitevin will die together at the same moment, having achieved nothing. Khalid-Morein proposes that he and Sudimentar switch lives with each other:

this is the only kind of dialectical conversion that can exist between individuals. Khalid-Morein also believes the remaining Artepoists should follow suit by exchanging their lives with one another, and he ventures instruction on a secret tantric ritual to effect such a metamorphosis (whose specifics only he is in possession of).

Flattery soon gives way to mortification – as it usually does – and Sudimentar ends up strangling Khalid-Morein for his impudent manuscript; the Artepoist is forced to surrender to the dawning realization that he cannot foresee chains of events outside the narrow remit of his hare-brained compositions; a break from a paradigmatic existence threatens, and a looming death not of his devising draws near. Left with little alternative, Sudimentar presents the body to the remaining Artepoists, prepared to stand revealed as a fraud. He submits to their judgment without a thought to his survival.

For mere moments, Sudimentar considers death by mob rule a glorious finish to his brief adventures in charismatic movement building. A ripple of reverent expectation washes over the Artepoists like morning dew. Frequent mention is made to the 'Parling of the Talebearer.' Sudimentar cannot place the term, though it sounds familiar. A fopling steps forward, and apprises Sudimentar of the section from his great master-work regarding an Artepoist being struck down by a higher power for his betrayal. Sudimentar remembers the passage now: he had been writing, perhaps in hindsight somewhat equivocally, about his landlady's garrulousness, and his hope that she fall out an open window.

The Artepoists redouble their unquestioning loyalty to Selworthy, while he in turn begins to understand that cheating death is not the antithesis of dying: the polarity of oblivion lies in creation. Selworthy has somehow expanded beyond the nanoscopic horizons of his writing on Lepoitevin; reality is conforming to his scripture at the same time that he is influencing the world around him, deviating from the path he has laid out for himself. In his mind, he has approached a mangy, dog-eared Godhood, becoming essentially a *prime mover*.

The uncertainty in *Artepoist* regarding Khalid-Morein's reservations about the achievability of the Sudimentarist/Artepoist project and its metafictional oversights is never resolved completely. This is further complicated by the fact that Sudimentar's sub-novel *Sudimentarism* ends with Artepo committing suicide with his lover in his arms, the same ending Lepoitevin supplies Sudimentar in *Artepoist*.

Swarthout

Lepoitevin was astounded by the reception of his book, which reached a kind of cult status within a year of its release. Budding writers wrote to him, pleading that he further expound this Sudimentarist principle in future works, or that he take them under his wing. He did both in fact, writing a total of ten Sudimentarist books in the course of his lifetime, and also establishing ten rotating spaces in his annual subscription-based school of Sudimentarist learning. This was how Artepo realized that he had transformed his arrangement of stylistic and narrative elements into a golden goose of financial wizardry.

To test this theory, Lepoitevin wrote a text that deviated from the arrangement in between Sudimentar Book 4 and Sudimentar Book 5, the much-maligned and forgettable *Swarthout*. It was of such monumental insignificance that Artepo's publisher initially believed he was trying to finagle advance money for a book that had not been written yet when he harassed them for royalty cheques. Nothing from *Swarthout* came to pass in Lepoitevin's life (it did not even contain Selworthy Sudimentar as a character). His Sudimentarist formula vindicated, he returned to Book 5 with rejuvenated confidence that Sudimentar's adventures in real-estate investment would redound to the Lepoitevin portfolio's credit (and it did, quite handsomely, I am told).

On the eve of the release of the eighth Sudimentar book, *Blatherwyrte*, a pupil named Elpenor Morein enrolled in Artepo's Sudimentarist writing program. Students bearing names of characters from his work were not uncommon; however, Artepo's investigations into this pupil bore no confirmation that a legal name change had occurred. Indeed, Elpenor claimed that he had only recently come across these books and wanted to enroll in the course to learn firsthand how Lepoitevin had come to christen Khalid-Morein.

It was the first time that the Sudimentarist movement faced a bona fide crisis. Fearing a usurper was in his midst, or that he'd have to follow Sudimentar's example to the letter thereby turning him into a murderer practically overnight, Lepoitevin became agitated with worry. Neither did he want to invite the consequences of a second divergence from the Sudimentarist path – he already felt that he had been playing with fire with *Swarthout*. Remembering Sudimentar's creed that godly creation was the path to beat back death's tromping advances, Lepoitevin took Elpenor as a confidante and lover, hoping to cheat death for a second time by skipping to the ending of *Artepoist*.

The Gonerhood of Kilmania

I will now leave off this subject for the moment, until its continuance is warranted by a discussion of Translassitude beyond its knobbled origins.

I became aware of *Artepoist* when it was recommended to me as an instructional tool by my friend, the writer and poet Behzad Molavi. I was promised that the novel contained several errors of an elementary nature, and I was persuaded to regard this text as productive to my own efforts by way of a cautionary measure: most of Lepoitevin's blunders were to be avoided at all costs.

I learned for one thing that self-bewitchment of one's intellectual labours was entirely the mark of a mountebank. I also gleaned the dangers of readers being over-reliant on the hermeneutic circle of understanding, couching readings of a text in its diversity of contexts (Translassists in point of fact believe it to be a hermeneutic *square*).

Artepoist was the most edifying text in this regard that I had ever encountered, and was always within reaching distance of my work table. I bought a few copies for my friends and peers in the profession. However, when I gave a copy to my associate Kilworthy Tanner, she assumed a look of intense, almost moronic deflation. I asked her if she owned a copy already, thinking at first that its duplication was the cause for her displeasure. She confirmed this and handed the book back to me uncivilly.

Kilworthy had been involved with someone, but had recently stepped out as a free agent, so I was disappointed that I had somehow allowed a misstep of this magnitude to come between us. I cursed the day that I had learned what an Artepoist was!

Kilworthy's breakout novel was called *Sugarelly*. It was about a woman who made a fabulous tar-like decoction in her bathtub and gave samples of the beverage to all the neighbours in her tenement building. The consumption of this 'sugarelly' allowed the tenants to experience sensational, life-affirming hallucinogenic wig-outs. They forswore their lives of corporate drudgery, abandoned their positions as accountants, bankers, and police officers for a life of poetry-composing, canvas-dotting, literature-mapping artistry. Unnerved by the loss of her identity amid the bedlam of uniformity, the woman killed each and every one of her neighbours with the wooden oar she used to stir the dread contents of her bathtub. The book was meant to be a veiled reworking of the rape of Dinah from the Book of Genesis. It was no difficult task to become obsessed with Kilworthy's destructive brilliance (or to want to be subjected to it).

I was so desperate to win her affections that I began poring over the snafu in my mind, and I came to realize that unless she was entirely hostile to the idea of receiving gifts from some-one she did not know very well (entirely conceivable), then it must be in my choice of token that upset her. All my efforts to see her again disintegrated. She broke off social engagements where she knew I would be present, but this cavalier attitude only contributed to my Kilmania. It is not a well-concealed secret that such patent spitefulness is the best way to lure me down the path of far gonerhood. I was completely besotted and diverted myself with guiles I could employ to persuade her to have me.

I turned to her assistant, Bedegraine Boisrond, for insight as to why Kilworthy had abruptly turned so cold. Boisrond confessed that she knew no reason, at least not any that she could put forward based on her employer's behaviour in the office. Boisrond had noticed that a sullenness had come over Kilworthy but adduced the change to one of the ungovernable moods to which the author was susceptible.

Bedegraine and I let the subject naturally expire, and passed the remainder of our lunch in good spirits discussing our respective projects. Upon settling the bill and accompanying her to her car, I noticed a book protruding from her purse. I asked if the book was beneath my notice. She pulled out the book and I made an alarming discovery. At first I believed Boisrond was reading an advance copy of Kilworthy's new novel, but as I had more time to scrutinize the cover, I realized that the book was in fact entitled *Kilworthy Tanner*, and that it was attributed to Artepo Lepoitevin. I could barely contain my shock and immediately directed a flurry of questions to Boisrond, apprising her that I had just the other day attempted to give Kilworthy a copy of *Artepoist*.

It was not long before I was caught up to speed and made aware of the reason for my ostracization; who would have thought that it boiled down to something as trivial as a paternal connection? Boisrond was forbidden from owning any Sudimentarist texts, much less the one based on Kilworthy's life. Boisrond was forced to read it only in the comfort of her home. She had reached the portion of the book concerning Kilworthy's first sexual partners, and she was certain that some of these individuals were still in her employer's life and had frequently made visits to the office; to confirm this, Boisrond had brought along a copy of the book on one occasion to compare with the records and correspondence at her disposal.

I immediately asked her how much she wanted for the book. Boisrond refused, citing the extreme difficulty she had in obtaining a copy, which had been published in extremely low numbers and never reprinted. It had cost her something in the neighbourhood of $500. I considered the impossibility of my finding another copy, weighed the social catastrophe of what I had planned and the probability that Boisrond would regale Kilworthy with the details of my indecorous actions without revealing the existence of the misappropriated text in question, and ran as fast and as far as my legs could carry me with Lepoitevin's Juvenal attack on his daughter still clenched in my hands.

Arcade of the Mind

I felt the direct approach best in this matter. I phoned Kilworthy and told her that I had a copy of the book her father had written about her. I apologized for giving her *Artepoist*, and confessed that I had not been privy to their relationship before offering it as a gift. I asked her to let me make amends for the gaucherie of the gesture, and she accepted, wanting to give an account of the reasons she had been treating me so coarsely.

We met the next morning for breakfast at P. J. Clarke's. In preparation for the meeting, I read as much of *Kilworthy Tanner* as possible, and brought the book along with me. It was Sudimentar's seventh book and better conceived than *Artepoist* by miles. I could not be certain if the book held my attention because of its subject matter, or because of the sense of mechanical anticipation that preceded every turn of the page, each revelation pregnant with sense-shattering disclosures that would amount to less than nothing for a lay reader. To my eyes, I found an ostensibly accurate accounting of Kilworthy's outlook, sensibilities, and attitudes on a handful of subjects. I could not begin to describe the humiliation one would endure to have something of this nature let loose into the world. The psychological implications alone were stupefying. I anticipated a meeting that would be a cross between awkwardness and embarrassment, the congenial environment I felt would best incubate my feelings of infatuation.

Kilworthy began speaking to me before I had time to properly seat myself and arrange my belongings: 'You'll not succeed in an undertaking to have me comment on any subject relating to that book. I don't want to see it, I don't want to discuss any of the particulars originating from my father's writing – not because it holds power over me, but because to acknowledge its insignificance is to set little store in my merits. I have erred by allowing the presentation of *Artepoist* to unsettle me. In so doing, I've not only insulted you, but I have done violence to my integrity. I am meeting with you today in an attitude of reclamation. I know you are interested in me sexually. I can't say that I feel the same or have been moved to arrive at the same conclusion. I give you permission to try to make good on these designs, but I do so indifferently and without anything but vague interest, and only until we have finished our three courses. If you are unsuccessful, you have to agree to our permanent standing as professional colleagues or face a complete severing of relations. Nod your head if you understand.'

I saw that the way to Kilworthy's heart was through her head, and staked my claim on those illumined corridors, the arcade of her mind. This subject coincides with the original question I posed of the inception of Translassitude: Kilworthy had long been considering a systematic response to her father's libellous creative output, which became the first topic of discussion over starters. The first task at hand had been to legally change her name from Tanner Lepoitevin into something that would both thumb her nose at Artepo's own alter ego and mockingly assert her corporeal desirability – in the way that men would kill and maim each other for the chance to date her.

The second order of the day was to obtain as many copies of *Kilworthy Tanner* as possible with the intent of destroying them before they could be made accessible forever, arriving at a digital permanence of sorts through the vastness of the Internet. So far she had succeeded on this front. I contributed to this worthy cause only after Kilworthy agreed to exchange the book for a Big Eight of cocaine and to look over the new work I was preparing, with the possibility of agreeing to blurb it if she enjoyed it (she did, and we celebrated a month later by doing rails of Charlie from each other's genitals).

Beyond the fact that using *Artepoist* as the gold standard of bad writing recommended me to Kilworthy's confidences, she could not resist the elucidative opportunity my reckless and unfocused writing afforded. She thought my work, upon familiarizing herself with it, was so starved for critical and popular recognition that I habitually made a spectacle of an otherwise average facility with language. I had previously never entertained the idea of receiving sexual satisfaction by having my life's work lambasted so thoroughly; paired with Kilworthy's flattering physical and mental arrangements, my fall into dissipation and degeneracy was nearly complete.

Implementation

Kilworthy's fledgling literary practices bore the distinctive markings of systematicity. I was the one who first suggested to her that the potential for widespread implementation exceeded what she had neatly envisioned for her books. Several of her insights had already been put into practice by writers of our ilk – Behzad Molavi, Cherelle Darwish, and Martin Zeilinger, to name a few. Kilworthy believed these associations diminished her accomplishments, but I propounded a beneficent reading to the observation, advancing that methodology was not only unavoidable but an expedient way to map one's extramundane impressions on the material world.

Every improvement of this as-yet-unnamed proficiency in the literary arts would embellish both her initiating and attendant achievements. My arguments overtook her reservations and she ceded to their validity, proposing we abuse ourselves using the sight of each other to bring the endeavour off to completion. Whoever expressed this secret vice more nimbly would have the onerous honour of naming the science we were developing. I know that she let me win this ridiculous contest, Kilworthy having since said something to the effect of how the sorry sight of an arthritic chandler did nothing to make the moment hum with carnal energy.

And unto Artepo was born Kilworthy, who begat Translassitude; and Translassitude lived for five years, and begat shame, ruin, and humiliation for all of its partisans.

Telegnosic Material Superiority and the Metaeffect

The basis for Translassitude bridges trials in converting my lethargic susceptibilities into high-yielding productive ends with Kilworthy's anti-gymnobiblism toward her father's bog-draining literary forays. I had long been attempting to solve for myself the problem of managing the creative impulse and its waning puissance, but without the requisite mental expenditure such a task would normally require. I needed all my solutions to amount to roughly the equivalent thought/application needed to scratch oneself. (Kilworthy here corrected my mistake with an epexegetic refinement to this idea – the equivalent thought/application to change out of *wet clothes*. There was nothing automatic about writing, and the analogy worked better if the utility of the act lay not in producing pleasure but in withholding discomfort.) And, on top of this, I refused to place stock in activities that did not confirm belief in my own genius. These two requirements having been gratified, Kilworthy and I were more than happy to lend our names publicly to the labours of Translassitude's parturition.

The idea then was to turn the involuntary consumptive gesture of looking into meaningful observation, but without forcing a taxing reaction from the physiological response systems. My first breakthrough was the resolve to submit all my behaviour to a process of sweeping categorization.

Dietary, socio-sexual, professional, illuminatory, musico-literary, and physical metrics helped me to valorize creative procedures operating at the many levels of consciousness, which were tiered in an ascending order of omnilassitude, paralassitude, and hyperlassitude. Although Kilworthy and I have never discussed it publicly, the oft-commented on and rumoured somnilassitude – the secret pinnacle of the Translassic system of literary science – *does* in fact exist.

The four phases of consciousness and their accompanying poetic properties are:

Omnilassitude: a state of non-categorization and vegetative lassitude that delights in the pleasures of the uncoordinated senses. Consciousness operates as a sensory medium absorbing uncorrupted data without altering its fundamental makeup. Such a state of consciousness is of no use to the Translassic purpose.

Paralassitude: a state of emerging categorization and occupied lassitude that operates with semi-coordinated sensory transparency. Consciousness acknowledges its operation as a cerebral medium corrupting data without altering the fundamental makeup of its information. Such a state of consciousness is of minimal usage to the Translassic purpose.

Hyperlassitude: a state of consolidated categorization and increased lassitude that operates with coordinated sensory optimality. Consciousness intentionally alters the fundamental makeup of its surroundings to effect material superiority of the environment. Such a state of consciousness is of optimal usage to the Translassic purpose.

Somnilassitude: a somni-state of instinctual categorization and equilibrative lassitude that operates with supra-optimal sensory proficiency. Consciousness no longer simply alters the fundamental makeup of its surroundings, but is able to develop multiple cascading sensory analysis to effect maximal material superiority of its environment. Consciousness is able to perceive its own processive metaeffect on material datums in both its alert and torpefied states of being. Such a state of consciousness is the only pure representation of the Translassic purpose, and can be turned to a telegnostic purpose.

Artepo-Slander

Before I describe the poetic corollaries to these conscious states, I want to devote a few lines to Kilworthy's unblemished system of Artepo-slander as I encountered it for the first time. It was further along in development than I presumed, amounting to a complex amalgamation of smear-campaigning, burlesque, and gossip-mongering, the likes of which had not been seen since the days of *Punch* and its brow-beating luminaries. Kilworthy employed a gallimaufry of autological concepts and rhetorical devicing, which was in turn undergirded by a staggering understanding of human psychological phenomena. She was single-handedly the best wielder of procatalepsis I have ever seen, totally inoculated from the moral disease of guilt.

Marshalling her hatred against a transgressor became the ultimate motivating principle for her writing. Writing was not about innovative conventions applied to theatrical and dramatic situations for cathartic release or aesthetic contemplation, but a *vaticination of the future*. She elucidated her father's suicide in the pages of *Variant* in more detail than *Artepoist* ever managed and even described the circumstances in which his body would be discovered: in the arms of a man half his age, also dead from an apparently self-inflicted wound from a serological pipette. It could be argued that her slanders and portraits of hideousness were coloured with the tincture of suggestible inescapability and that their intended targets felt utterly compelled to follow through on Kilworthy's projections.

Lay Low the Lovels and Boontueanthabs of the World

There are two other cases where Kilworthy was able to influence, forecast, or motivate individuals to do her bidding.

In the case of Lovel Focillon, her first husband, Kilworthy released the novel *Flintskin* eighteen months prior to his arrest for assault and battery in a South Stormont brothel, where he was also charged for forging *spintriae* in mass numbers. Sasithorn Boontueanthab suffered a similar fate when she was accurately identified as being the basis of the titular character in Kilworthy's fourth novel. Kilworthy's goal with Sasithorn had long been to persuade her to abandon a career in writing, and though this has not been proven definitively, Boontueanthab has not published anything since the public outing.

Boontueanthab's prose was of an unadorned and lyrical variety, and as such Kilworthy had no reason to feel threatened by her rival's artistic projects. The two writers, however, seemed to be working toward the same thematic bearing, with their books often developing in parallel, either by design or the intervention of fate. It was Boisrond in fact who had discovered the truth by stumbling into Boontueanthab's office at a dinner party held at her home. It was decorated with multiple copies of Kilworthy's books that had been pored over and copiously overburdened with notes. On the strength of this occurrence alone, Kilworthy went to work at levelling the borrowed foundations of Boontueanthab's first water reputation.

Kilworthying

A curious feature of Kilworthy's process was her use of the palimpsest as a cladistic tool of writing. She would take to scrivening entire passages from *Artepoist* with the intent of familiarizing herself with her father's frame of mind and stylistic voice. She would follow this exercise with acts of delicate subversion. Words would be redrafted to obfuscate or clarify meaning and intention, both to understand the correct apportioning of the poetic functions within the original text and to undermine them. When Kilworthy became comfortable with this exercise of imitation, she would move on to rewriting the entire passage, first in a way that preserved its initial function, improved it, and then in a way that annihilated it. She called this process of textual erosion 'kilworthying.'

Once she had assembled a handful of these passages from *Artepoist*, and much later on, Boontueanthab's *Trilby Psychic*, Kilworthy would begin the next stage of active composition by reading over the source passage, putting it aside, and rewriting the text from memory. She would then put all these passages side by side and choose the worst of the lot (Kilworthy did not determine a passage's shoddiness on any logical basis – she would simply come to think of it as inferior or deficient by gut-divining its merits). These sabotaged passages would become the substructure of her work in progress, and she would fashion them into a loose structural outline. She had filed away over fifty of these *débauches* of existing works, which she would later resurrect when it came time to begin new assignments. She made a point to never use any outline before a year had elapsed from its date of creation.

The next phase involved soliciting the opinion of her assistant. For five years, this dubious honour had fallen to Bedegraine Boisrond. Boisrond would pick a *débauche* at random or after scanning through titles, and Kilworthy would tackle the project if she approved of the composition. Kilworthy's previous assistants had never lasted more than a year or so because of their ineptness in selecting acceptable *débauches* – Kilworthy did not start remunerating them for their services until they picked a productive candidate, which was based on a graduated scale dependent on whether the completed book won awards, the ratio of good to bad reviews, and final book sales.

Boisrond held the record of being in Kilworthy's employ the longest of any assistant, and her salary was rumoured to exceed six figures, due to her hidden flair for reading her employer's mind. A much simpler reasoning, of course, for their continued professional arrangement, was that Kilworthy simply liked Boisrond and made justifications for her continued employment, which made Boisrond's seditious possession of Sudimentarist texts all the more irreconcilable.

What I found most appealing about Kilworthy's long-drawn-out and venturesome writing exertions was their superfluous and ritualistic nature, marrying the natural impulses of both obsessive order and mayhem. I wanted to maintain both of these creative resolutions, but I also wanted to put some distance between them. To do this, I asked Kilworthy whether or not it would be possible to recalibrate her stages of writing in a way that limited the amount of extraneous composition, overdeveloping what Boisrond's culling-and-selection process essentially represented without involving any assistants directly. I believed that after more than fifty instances of completed palimpsestic exercises, Kilworthy's method of para-writing should be an instinctual process at this point, not unlike her father's own abandonment of figure studying and toning canvases in the last stages of his painting career before adopting Sudimentarism.

I wanted to see the results and consequent mental liberation that might ensue from Kilworthy applying the philosophy of croquis drawing to her writing; more than anything, I wanted

us into a moment of Translassic perception, which we would later term 'quail-piping' – dissolving a hit of LSD back and forth between our lips while boxing tonsils, but with the novel benefit of being so weary from our sleep and food regimen that we could fall asleep before coming up on whatever drugs we had been ingesting. One had to get 'unstuck' to welcome a depersonalization process that would align consciousness with nontranscendence. In other words, could human consciousness become a being-in-itself?

The Hermeneutic Square

We had our work cut out for us, but we were certain that our heightened sensitivity to epistemological processes and perceptual changes would lead us to only the surest conclusions, the most adamantine of discoveries.

Schematizing the four states of Translassitude became a constitutive task when we began formalizing narrative corollaries to the hermeneutic square: omnilassitude with an exploratory stage (*deployment*) called the parametrics of obscurity/paraobscurmetric pole, paralassitude with a clarified stage (*consolidation*) called the parametrics of significance/parasignimetric pole, hyperlassitude with an autotelic stage (*expansion*) called the parametrics of diversion/paradivermetric pole, and finally somnilassitude with an impredicative and paralogical stage (*teleological purification*) called the parametrics of purity/parapurimetric pole.

Unlike the Sudimentarists, who strove for total dialectical subsumption of a subdominant persona to a dominant one (the single rotation of a hermeneutic circle), Translassists believe that movement between the four quadrants of the hermeneutic square are dialogic in nature: transition and activity between the four stages, and in any order – once a full rotation has occurred, of course – is not prohibited.

If omnilassitude can be considered the native state of a purely absorptive, non-productive consciousness, then the passage into paralassitude (whether in tandem with quail-piping or some other *recherché* method) coincides with the Translassist's first forays into artistic creation, deploying a burgeoning ensemble of themes, images, and scenarios that betrays the sensibilities and discursive tics that will characterize their future output.

Paralassitude, and the concomitant awareness of the flood of new sensory information pouring into a Translassist's consciousness, brings about the consolidation of technical formalist preoccupations into a stable and clarified system of narrative conventions.

The progression from paralassitude into hyperlassitude is a mindful leap forward into autotelism, and while not wholly revisionist in nature, does pivot around the recalibration of paralassitude's principal consolidation of elements; the exemplary nature of paralassic output is made more exemplary, with dynamic but limited experimentation to these texts' tradition-alisms. What makes the hyperlassic state and texts autotelic is the fact that expansion is effectively curbed and has reached its limit. Paralassitude's classicism has merged with hyperlassitude's neo-classicism, if you will.

Intimations of the purported final state of Translassitude have hitherto been shrouded in the most artificially maintained secrecy. We take full responsibility for the apocryphal Trans-lassist texts attributed to Aldegonde Ste. Croix, which we released for the express purpose of befogging the inner pathways of Translassic lifework. I can now reveal that this eruptive and recursive form of consciousness does exist.

What quail-piping was to the emergence into paralassitude, so *power-pixing* helped usher our entry into the elevated condition of somnilassitude (we added an eight ball to the quail-pipe mix). Writing under the somnilassic state is essentially communion with the unconscious mind under the instruction and behest of the hypethral *phren*. Under the phren's somni-tutelage, the latent content of all material data is tethered to the morotrophium of the Translassic purpose: in short, composition becomes possible while asleep.

A deliberate jiggering of the assumed arrangement between paralysis and activity enables us to coordinate reception of sensory stimuli while immobilized by rest. Brain activity retains the ability in its anabolic state to marshal speech and occasionally even direct the hand to record fragmentary sentences or salient ideas in the form of mnemonic trigger words. The somnilassic state, however, is not beholden to the ultimate principles of dream logic; just as theta wave activity has been linked with the waking state and dream states alike, one can surmise that under the right training – a vernalization process if you will – one can make use of the many parametrics at play in the related disciplines of oneirology, transcendental homelessness, authorial intentionalism, etc.

The Parametrics of Purity

The parametrics of purity is at its core an imitative and referential faculty. The literary productions written in this state of consciousness take on a paralogical quality. Paralogism does not in this regard mean untenability or basis in fallacy; the paralogism refers to the break from the generative orthodoxy of hyperlassitude and the parameters of diversion. This is what we mean by teleological purification: somnilassitude represents a recusant mindset, resisting the idea that hyperlassitude is the absolute limit of expressive conceivability. If there is to be a limit to the evolutionary movement of creative endeavour and artistic output, it can never lie in the frontierspace of knowable boundaries. At the last perceptible edge of any unilateral progression comes the *anti-mythic reversal*, the impredicative temptation to look in the opposite direction and turn in on itself, flanking the path of floridity and flamboyance, bedizening its instrumentation and mechanics with self-reference – we have entered, in short, the domain of satire and the metatext.

Kilworthy and I believe the parametrics of purity must be used sparingly. The physiological cost alone of entering the somnilassic state of consciousness is prodigious. Side effects whose relative permanence is not conclusively known include short- and long-term memory loss, decrease of libidinal sensitivity, incontinence, personality disruption, numbness in the extremities, nausea, existential malaise, drug addiction, increased susceptibility to pleasurable experiences, and in the rarest of cases, a tendency and inability to resist repetition in structuring plots (in my own case, rewriting novels over and over again in a locked tangle of mental stagnation).

My experiences with writing under the somnilassic condition have usually been disastrous. I have succeeded in bringing off only one story for publication, the vulgarity exhibition known as 'Swiddenworld,' which is based on letters exchanged between Kilworthy and me, and recordings of our conversational somni-snorings. It is quite possible to create metatexts and satirical texts while in the wakeful state, of course, but this is not advised. For one thing, an author cannot resist giving full spleen to their cleverness and will often find themselves a tough row to hoe – they do not know when to bring their cogitations to heel, and are unable to gauge the degree to which folly will guide the griffonage against enemies and barbarians alike, proving just how behindhand we can be in paying back the debt of scornful abuse. The beauty of the somnilassic spleen is it oscillates in roughly equal measure between repleteness and privation, and is by far the best touchstone for balance in scholarly avocations.

Satire written outside of the parapurimetric order also runs into the trouble of rendering judgments that are incomplete, on the basis of parochial implements of observation. This was certainly the case with Lepoitevin's *Kilworthy Tanner*, whose pretensions to arguteness clearly fell short of the mark, in no small part due to the incommodious persona of being a father. One must adopt a holistic, bordering on omniscient, view to the proceedings, becoming father, lover, brother, sister, mother, friend, and enemy alike, and this is made viable only through the somnilassic order of parametric purity, risking bathetic outturns and unintended reactions to an otherwise sound gestative intellectual undertaking.

Failure, under the right circumstances, behooves Translassists, allows them to right the course of a never-ending expedition through the conceptual heights of the mental plane. Translassitude is not a point of arrival or departure but a liquidation of archaic thoughtforms shackled to the distraction dimension of time. Movement through and to the past, present, and future is not possible via an iterative Sudimentarist loop; only a reciprocating psycholinguistic frame of consciousness that cycles abundantly through the modalities of mental qualia and its propositional attitudes can make a positive outcome likely.

Draffsacker

One aggregative method toward the pansophic parametrics of purity is via somni-rapport with another parapurimetric mind. Thus far, Translassists have identified only a handful of these acroamatic measures, such as the *somni-fuck* and the choral *somni-snore* (more mellifluous designations for these placeholders have yet to be finalized). But these exercises are mere preludes to the active work that must take place during the waking hours of consciousness – the hours of play while cycling through parasignimetric and paradivermetric advertency. Because we hoped to mobilize whatever lingering draff of parapurimetric consciousness remained in the early hours of metabolic awakening, Kilworthy and I devised an ingenious approach to drafting novels called *draffsacking* – we have elsewhere termed it *Jack Abeling*, after the American inker/embellisher who was known as a first-rate background artist for comic strips.

One of Kilworthy or myself would take lead on a novel and write the book out as a series of introductory paragraph sentences; in instances where more instruction was needed, concluding sentences often followed. The point of this operation was to expend as much somnilassic mileage as possible before its effects began to wear off. The draffsacker would follow the instruction of the lead writer and fill in the necessary detail between these sentences, subject to review at a later interval. This allowed a novel to participate in somnilassitude as much as was physically possible. The draffsacker would never receive official credit for these efforts, because Translassists believe occasional abasement in the name of a higher good to be productive of creative honesty and fearlessness. The lead writer would be able to rewrite the draffsacker's contributions at will, thus maintaining Kilworthy's exhaustive bathymetric and hypsometric standardizations of annihilating the written word.

Another literary technique we have become particularly notorious for is the much misunderstood process of *tuyèring*. Detractors believed it to be a completely empty concept to disguise the fact that I allegedly never planned out novels or used outlines. This is in fact false. Translassic books were organized around what we called a 'winch chapter,' which would be composed under an aleatory framework of breathable, spontaneous improvisation. This chapter could be placed in any part of a book, provided progressive chapters deferred to the winch chapter's internal logic and momentum without qualification. I preferred to situate them almost exclusively at the beginning of books, whereas Kilworthy unorthodoxly placed them in the middle or near the end. The idea was for the text to bloom organically and leave room for discovery and innovation during the drafting process. Once a text was complete, one could make the necessary adjustments needed to firm up thematic concerns that would begin to dominate the work through a movement of ingenerate profusion.

Lovedumping the Drip

Naturally, we cannot go into more than rudimentary detail about these four frames of consciousness or the vast array of literary concepts at our disposal; it would not stand with faithful subscribers and lifelong adherents to the Translassic egregore, to say nothing of increasing the probability of Translassitude being further misunderstood outside the walls of our organization. Thus ends the abridgment of the Translassic core thymology for the remainder of this monograph.

What we are at liberty to discuss at this juncture is the revived attention to the question of under which parametric systems or frames of consciousness Kilworthy and I have composed our books. These are not nugatory inquiries of an inappreciable nature, and may serve to expound some of the more arcane features of these respectable works.

Grand Menteur was written under a state of hyperlassic consciousness and the parametrics of diversion – it was draff-sacked by Kilworthy. *In the Beggarly Style of Imitation* was written under a state of paralassic consciousness and the parametrics of significance, though initial forays into somnilassic consciousness were attempted ('Swiddenworld,' 'Sentiments and Directions from an Unappreciated Contrarian Writer's Widow'). *Kilworthy Tanner* (my version) was my first attempt to run laps around the hermeneutic square *in public* while writing under a singular narrative voice.

For her part, Kilworthy's Translassic output began with the paralassic *Love Dump*, and the hyperlassic *Decretals of Minge* (draffsacked by myself) and ended with the fully Translassic *Drippydick* (unknown if draffsacked at all), a 200-page pasquinade of my genitals after she discovered I had begun a friendship with her father and had witnessed a sexual initiation rite involving Artepo's new muse, the ex-Translassist Aldegonde Ste. Croix, in order to become acquainted with the inner light of Sudimentarism (attributing the act's agency to Serge Mayacou, a character from one of my novels whom I had been attempting to Sudimentarize, did not go over well with Kilworthy).

Kilworthy has broken off and renounced Translassitude completely, severing all usage of the techniques and protocols we conceived together. I find this difficult to believe, since more than half of the system's features were based on Kilworthy's own incursions into the soul's flocculating passageways. At any rate, Kilworthy continues to cash my cheques accounting for her half of all revenues deriving from Translassic activity that is not currently being contributed back into the movement and allocated as an outlay for its continued subsistence.

Transmentar

My direct acquaintance with Artepo Lepoitevin began when the Translassitude Society received a letter of intent to sue from the disgraced Sudimentarist, which included a settlement demand in the amount of $250,000. I did not want to nettle Kilworthy, wanting to spare her the aggravation by handling the matter as privately as possible. I went to meet Artepo at a restaurant on Orchard Street in the Lower East Side, where he put paid to many of my assumptions regarding his character and state of mind. He certainly did not act like someone who was asking for a quarter of a million dollars, which I most certainly did not have. He played the part of the reprobate ironically, and made no mention of Sudmentarism or his daughter until I broached the subject myself.

He organized his arguments from largest to small, beginning with the appropriation of Sudimentarist curriculae for use in our Translassic synods, followed by defamatory remarks made in several Translassic publications and encyclicals, and ending on the allegation that he was the basis for the character of Artepo Lepoitevin in several of my stories. I could not deny this last accusation, but made by way of reply an enquiry into what I had written that was factual and what was perhaps unintelligible conjecture.

'You wrote it in the beggarly style of Translassic imitation – this is all that matters,' he began. 'You made me realize that a Translassic Sudimentarism would be very much inevitable in the future fullness of time. Can you not be given to understand that it would be something worth pursuing?'

We discussed, at first coyly, then with diminishing reserve, what we saw to be the chief hindrances to our systems' functionability, then quickly moved on to the subject of our legacy-building objectives. Solutions that did not revolve around Translassitude or Sudimetarism all pointed to schism and fragmentation, whereas the resolutions afforded by our two votive indoctro-systems always lead to affirmation, belief, and authentication. This species of opportunity seldom knocks lightly or in accordance with so-called ethical ordinances. My decision was made before we parted ways that night. A Translassic-Sudimentarism, or a *Transmentarism*, was not just possible, but a practical inexorability; one does not fight time any more than one fights elemental ruin. I also realized that my failure to anticipate the legal entanglements with Artepo invalidated the prognosticating features of somnilassitude to a degree; I shared Sudimentar's own realization all those years ago that we could be caught off guard by events in which we had little hand but desperately sought to control. We shook on having become brother Transmentars, welcoming both the changes to raiment and behaviourisms.

I broke the news in as straightforward a fashion as I could with Kilworthy. We had grown distant these past months for one reason or another – jealousy, overfamiliarity, passivity resulting from detachment – but we still had no secrets between us. She looked at me as if I had confirmed her worst fears, had fouled the nest, and taken a large stake to her heart, carving it into morsels before serving it to dogs, the animals she reviled the most of any other. I was not prepared for the ferocity of her rebukes against me. I believed I could compartmentalize the impending synthesis between Sudimentarism and Translassitude, keeping Kilworthy to one side of the affair, but I was *very* much mistaken.

She wanted no part of the arrangement naturally. I should have anticipated this, but my mind was clouded with the possibilities before Artepo and me. Transmentarism could not serve as a paltry literary science ennobling future generations of writers; it had to now give succour to the less fortunate and become a *political instrument*.

Circle Squared

Built into the very foundation of Sudimentarism was the need for janissaries and dyads, the moulting of rotational identities, and a pathological fear of the unwritten future; written into the bones of its being, Translassitude triangulated psychogenic mental phenomena and used hortatory aptitudes to convert this data into a literary system that optimized existence. The political dimension was obvious – Transmentarism was an apodiptic system of control before it had even come into being. All that was left was to point it in a direction of our choosing.

Before this undertaking could begin in earnest, Artepo strongly cautioned me that there was one last order of business that needed attending. We needed to test that Transmentarism could still function as a nonpareil literary apparatus. There was nothing the electorate despised more than an unfledged candidate who had not excelled in their home profession. Paradoxically, we could also not rest on the laurels of our respective achievements when entering the political arena, but needed to deliver new tangible proofs of our intentions and achievements: our heredity and filiation.

There had been no Transmentarist novel to date. What might it look like? What would its effects produce? What would its relationships of hostility and symmetry be with other texts? I confess I did not fully appreciate the thinking behind it, considering we were about to embark on a political odyssey (unless its royalties were meant to finance the experiment …).

I was at a loss at what direction to take. My first test as a Transmentarist and I had apparently failed. Artepo put a hand steadily on my shoulder and told me that the answer, like any worth knowing, was under my nose the entire time.

'The heart of Sudimentarism, the soul of Translassitude, has always been Tanner,' he said gravely. 'What did she do after I disowned her? What do you think she will do to you, if she has not started months ago already, foretelling as she always does your wandering, inconstant eye? Her mind turns with ideas of the adaptive reuse of your skull. We must avoid the detractive effect of whatever libellous tome she releases in your honour. Now is the time to circle the square, Jean Marc – you must Sudimentarize my daughter.'

New Word Order

The difficulties before me were daunting. Kilworthy wanted no part of the campaign Artepo and I were developing, so I had to make a choice that would have far-reaching social consequences. Kilworthy, to her credit, did not force an ultimatum on me. Instead, she merely waited for an answer. A month after entertaining Artepo's offer to join forces, I moved out of Kilworthy's Ludlow Street studio and moved back to Canada to live in Artepo's commune. She released *Drippydick* six months later. The need for a Transmentarist response became more essential than ever.

Artepo and I held talks with various big wheels in the political arena, consulted with donors who had a foot in both the literary and policy-making worlds, and soon began to work in earnest on drafting a platform to announce the arrival of Transmentarism to various constituencies. Concurrent to these efforts was the early planning stages of my new book, which would have me assume Kilworthy's mind and bring the first public act of Transmentarism into narrative fruition: the aforementioned *Kilworthy Tanner*.

Our first impulse was to consolidate our already sizable political base. Besides introverts and literary types, Translassitude and Sudimentarism had amassed no shortage of lumpen political undesirables all too willing to do our bidding in the service of a higher aspirational calling. The first Transmentarist work would have to give these followers a lifestyle worth emulating, and a motive to alter their states of consciousness through the hermeneutic square as the political situations they rapidly found themselves in demanded. Most strikingly, we would no longer be encouraging our liegemen and liegewomen to compose their own emulatory texts.

Transmentarism departed from its primogenitors by offering mobility where there was previously stagnation, susceptibility to autonomic suggestion where there had been previously limber individualism (Transmentarists are especially susceptible to instruction when recovering from a somnilassic frame of mind). Transmentarism subsumed its members under the broader cultural ukase of enlightenment for all, leaving behind the paltry and more immediate ambitions of solipsistic personal advancement. Transmentarists would be classed into action groups, and deployed in accordance with the inner machinations of the Transmentarist *geist*. Sudimentarism had made success and fortune for its members; now spiritually starved, they craved something of true substance to enrich the hollow pantomimes parading about as their lives.

The most significant feature of Transmentarism would be its limit-skirting imitative capability – Transmentarists could fully embody another individual's thought processes, artistic ability, politics, behaviours, and habits as much as was humanly possible. It was even attainable from this artificial vantage point – that of the assumed identity, the *blatherwyrte* – to Transmentarize yet another individual. In other words, a Transmentarized identity could blatherwyrte an untold number of individuals, pending their cognitive capacity and overall physical constitution.

If he so desired, Artepo could Transmentarize myself, and from the relay of a Transmentarized Jean Marc Ah-Sen, Transmentarize Kilworthy Tanner, and further along one of Kilworthy's new lovers, *ad infinitum*, if he did not lose his bottle or mind in the process. On record, we have gone as far as seven degrees of relayed consciousness – Artepo currently holds this record-breaking distinction.

The great error with Translassitude was that Kilworthy and I deemed ourselves the lone cartographers of the Translassic mindscape and believed with unflinching conviction that we were the caretakers of this science. With Transmentarism, Artepo and I would leave the final end unrealized – this was an entelechial journey to be experienced by the total unbroken knot of Transmentarist praxeologists. We would walk into the pneuma-capped vistas of the mind together or not at all. The immediate political and artistic end was to produce a work that was virtually indistinguishable from that of a blatherwyrted individual. Anything beyond this goal was a matter for tuyèring on a cosmological level to handle.

Artepo was worried that an awakened political consciousness unaware of what it had awakened to would be cause for communal disintegration. To that purpose, I recruited Bedegraine Boisrond, Sasithorn Boontueanthab, and Lovel Focillon as consultants to help systematize our replicative efforts and tackle this participatory problem. They shared my belief that eternal rewards are more engaging if left to the imagination of the beholder. More importantly, the presence of Boisrond, Boontueanthab, and Focillon helped buttress my daily interaction with ex-Sudimentarists and ensured my voice would not become lost in the rasping ululations of the Transmentarist ensemble. They girdled my person as I moved from one corner of Artepo's commune to the other, and also directed my efforts in the most pressing matter at hand: bending the esoteric photon flow of Kilworthy's froth-lined inner light toward the surface.

Instead we completed an economic tract and called it *The People's Way Forward into Forever*, slapping on the cover the candidate's face who seemed the most inclined to champion these ideas. We circulated complimentary copies at gatherings on both sides: one to lift up, the other to tear down. The charade was not immediately discovered by the candidate to whom the text was attributed; it took some time for high-ranking politicos to realize a game was afoot in their backyard. Elpenor confirmed when the party became fully aware of the forgery. They did not want to denounce its credibility outright for fear of looking weak: weak through infiltration, and weak through obtuseness for not carrying their own ideas to their logical conclusions (vegetarianism, Ludditism, nudism, scato-barbarism).

This was the most opportune moment for contact. We anonymously introduced ourselves via letter, and were outrageously ridiculed for the effort. The candidate won the election in no small part due to our actions, and we have not had any of our subsequent correspondence returned. We attempted to lay low this contemptible politician by releasing an ode to pederasty in his blatherwyrted hand, but our efforts were stymied at the printing level when the books were due for publication. We suspect political interference from a high level (perhaps by the grand federal poobahship himself), and even consider the possibility of an infiltrator in our midst not unlikely (I had Elpenor and Aracy whipped to be certain). We may have further meddlesome individuals of influence to contend with.

Moreover, the newly incorporated Transmentarist Group is being investigated by the Canada Revenue Agency for financial irregularities in our business filings. The political rivals of the Pederasty party have expressed interest in obtaining the pede-slander book, but in exchange for the vague promise of future political favours, citing conciliatory influence on any potentially catastrophic financial investigations into our communal settlement. I fear we may have overstepped our bounds in this emprise, having incited a war on two power fronts of thimblerigging activity. Now that you are abreast of our failure to avoid the political bad beat, I hereby invoke articles 05-18 and 06-17 of the Transmentarist Constitution and recite the Sunset Ablation Clause in its entirety –

Ablation March of the Apex Mentarist

'Kilworthy Tanner,' I hereby summon you to the Citadel of the Spirit, our base of operations, and request the commencement of the Ablation March. I recall your cognintelligence backward to the paraobscurmetric pole, and ask that Madame Boisrond make the necessary arrangements to receive your return there. Once you are of sound body and mind to resume the affiliated responsibilities of the Apex Mentarist, I will renounce the parapurimetric pole of 'Jean Marc Ah-Sen' to you and assume my place by your side as your draffsacker, Artepo Lepoitevin, for what little moments remain my own. I have grown ill in your absence and am not long for this earth. Your time spent researching Kilworthy's life must come to an end. If you have not found the answers you seek through assuming the imprint of her writing and so too the imprint of her mind, all is well. Take heart – the experiment is not lost. My time Transmentarizing the Ah-Sen positrons of being have been a resounding success.

I have Transmentarized one of your existing manuscripts, obliterating several key passages and rearranging the sequencing of the chapters of your autobiographical micro-sketch collection. I have secured offers for publication from two interested parties. You have only to review the contract stipulations and sign off on them. In many instances, I have undone the groundwork Kilworthy laid in her draffsacking: I 'Selworthied' the manuscript, to coin a phrase. I gave the novel a conciliatory ending to gall Kilworthy's ego; her original finale was a prurient and sensational finale to a book already overloaded with sensationalisms. There is currently no popular appetite among readership for patricide and necro-vilification. Should you approve of these alterations and additions, we will have tangible proofs of the Transmentarist method.

You will have to wait a few months after its publication before revealing the true nature of its composition, but you will find the book indistinguishable from your past offerings – only if your readership believes the same will we have validated our transimitative enterprise, whatever its final purpose turns out to be. The publication of this monograph, *Parametrics of Purity*, will serve as its final, vindicating proof.

I will have Transmentarized your life and bloated it with my Sudi-structures, will have come about an artistic statement congruent with your grey eminence. Transmentarism will be proven as a discrete facsimile writing service to authors, politicians, and slanderers alike, and soon our depleted coffers will runneth over once more. It would be unwise to reveal a complete client list of texts we will have blatherwyrted for profit. Whenever a book is written whose sentiments don't entirely conform with its author's oeuvre, when an inconsistent admission is given or a reader taken into embarrassing confidences, people will wonder: Do I hold a Transmentarist text in my hands? Has some such figure been blatherwyrted from afar and for silver?

For the time being, our primary goal must be in rebuilding our finances and rebuffing any razzias on our livelihoods, never mind whatever embryonic political ambitions we may have once harboured. We will heed this call, whatever the cost.

I have thereby completed all requirements of the Transmentarist prolegomenon, effecting the transfer of powers in accordance with our irrebuttable protocols. The reputability of this document is indisputable, conforming to the concordat between us that laid out conditions for extraction and retrieval in perilous times of crisis, ablating aeroembolisms of abreactive thoughtforms from another life, another time. I have confirmed this intention from the mnemonic object trigger of my White Light Technician Thinking Throne (the main level lavatory of the Citadel).

I offer as my final indemnification against charges of forgery, surrendered freely and without coercion, the following testament: I hereby name my daughter, 'Kilworthy' Tanner Lepoitevin, as my financial and spiritual heir to all monies, assets, and properties belonging to and in the name of the Sudimentarist School of Learning, to use as she sees fit in the maintenance of the goals and responsibilities of the Transmentarist Group. I do so on the basis of bridging the impassable gap between my children, Tanner Lepoitevin and Jean Marc Ah-Sen, who should not be kept apart because of the indiscretions and miscalculations of my life.

Vulputate

There are no existing preconditions that must be satisfied in order to effect this transfer of powers and authority, now that the lustration of my Artepoism is complete. I must hearken to the *appel du vide* that has been racking my soul since I first encountered the hypno-realists – Elpenor and I must join Sudimentar in the gathering dust of the incorporeal planes before the ravages of my illness can incentivize young blatherwyrtes with vigilance and heedfulness – Sudimentarist sins all – and tempt them with a recrudescence of tangential book-billowing and scribble-romps. Please bring along a pipette of Kilworthy's mixture of quebrachine for my refreshment in the afterlife. We are about to do violence to our integrity (on a toilet no less …) in an attitude of reclamation. Nod your head if you understand. Let our deaths be our own, and incarnated as they were always meant to be: vulturine monstrosities of unconstraint, Artepoists one and all.

Etaoin!

Shrdlu!

Artepoist!

The Green Notebook

Devon Code

Foreword

The text presented here originated as a series of numbered notes handwritten in pencil in a hardcover notebook found in the author's study. Though the entries are undated, several references indicate they were written during the period directly preceding her death. Both their form and content constitute a significant departure from her later analytically oriented works, *The Human Language* and *Double Slit*, and a return to the more speculative and autobiographical *The Tardy Harbinger* and *Be That As It May*. On the final page appears a list of titles the author had either recently read or intended to read: Kuhn's *Structure of Scientific Revolutions*, Dunkley's *Our Universe*, Arendt's *Life of the Mind* and *The Origins of Totalitarianism*, Wittgenstein's *Tractatus Logico-Philosophicus*, Benatar's *Human Predicament* and *Better Never to Have Been*, Heisenberg's *The Physical Principles of the Quantum Theory*, and Frankl's *Man's Search for Meaning*. There is no indication the author intended the content of this notebook for publication. It is presented here in hopes it may inspire a new generation of thinkers who share her concern with the reduction of unnecessary suffering.

1.00] To live is to suffer.

1.01] Suffering may provide one with a source of meaning though it is not the only source. This is Frankl's insight.

1.02] Suffering involves a complex interplay of the physical and psychological.

1.03] Awareness of the imminence of one's death may increase one's suffering or else alleviate it, for death means the necessary end of one's suffering, including the suffering that the knowledge of one's imminent death may exacerbate.

1.04] In recent centuries we have made great advances in the physical sciences. At the same time, advances in the organization of our societies so as to eliminate unnecessary collective and individual suffering have been either inadequate or counterproductive.

1.05] A failure in our attempt to organize our societies humanely has led to movements in the physical sciences being used against our own collective prosperity, for movement must proceed in one direction or another, and in the absence of the possibility of moving forward, the movement becomes lateral or else regressive.

2.00] When one reflects on one's career and thinks about the opportunities one has missed, one realizes what has really been required all along is a rethinking of the relationship between the physical sciences and the social sciences, between physical space and psychological space.

2.01] As one's body slowly starts to fail, one's mind seizes on the possibility that modes of understanding originating in the physical sciences can be applied to the psychological in order to reduce unnecessary suffering. These modes of understanding can be applied at the level of both the individual and the collective.

2.02] The greatest challenge in one's relations with others is to understand others as they are. The first step toward understanding others is to correctly gauge the psychic distance between them and one's self. Without knowing the precise distance between one and others, one cannot hope to overcome this distance, for others will remain foreign objects at indeterminate remove.

2.03] For too long we have been attempting to calculate the psychic distance between one's self and others using a faulty methodology. Just as Huygens once attempted to calculate the distance of the stars by comparing their respective brightnesses, assuming all stars radiated the same brightness and their respective brightness or dimness was merely a matter of their proximity to the Earth, we have been making similarly incorrect assertions about the nature of others, assuming that certain facets of people are uniform when in fact they are multivalent. Our resulting attempts to ascertain and overcome the psychic distance between one and the other have thus been unsuccessful.

2.04] Instead one must employ the methodology of *socio-parallax* to gauge one's psychic distance from others, relying on multiple vantage points of perception and the reliable constant of a relatively stable societal backdrop. Just as an astronomer may measure the distance of a celestial body by first observing from Earth the other celestial body's position against the fixed reference point of a distant backdrop of stars and then observing its position against the frame of reference once again six months later when the Earth in its orbit has travelled to the opposite side of the sun, so may one calculate one's psychic distance from the other by using a comparable methodology. One may, by observing an other from two distinct psychic vantage points with a known distance between them, calculate the psychic distance to said other by using the distant backdrop of society as a fixed point of reference. One must only make note of the position of the other in relation to society in the first vantage point, then note the comparative distance of the other from the second vantage point. The application of this more accurate methodology has multiple implications for determining what has heretofore been unknowable about interrelations between one and an other. With this new and deeper knowledge of one another, the distances between one and an other must no longer limit the relationship to dynamics of fear, dominance, and subjugation.

3.00] Just as one may come to know the elemental composition of a distant star by refracting its light through a prism into its spectrum of colours and analyzing the signature of its spectral lines, so too may one discern the psychological intricacies of individuals and their collectives through prisms of consciousness. One need only view individuals and their collectives with a discerning eye through the methodology of *psychological spectrometry*. In this way one may compare the unknown with the known and render the unknown knowable. This knowledge dissipates fear, and a new way of relating emerges.

3.01] What if it comes down to a case of one's suffering or the suffering of the other? What if a little suffering of the other alleviates much of one's own suffering? These distinctions between one and an other are misleading, as are our attempts to judge the quality and quantity of suffering.

4.00] Direct sunlight has recently become an affront to one's eyes. One must keep the shade partially drawn on cloudless afternoons. One derives some solace in the knowledge that most of the universe's mass is composed of dark matter, which exists and exerts its influence everywhere but does not absorb or emit light and remains inscrutable. So too are human affairs determined by the dark forces of desire and compulsion, the presence of which can be deduced through careful observation but never explained nor fully understood. Just as vast and complex webs of dark matter resembling neural networks bind our universe together, the unfathomable psychic impulses of compulsion undergird human society. The particles of desire that collectively comprise the dark content of our unconscious are five times denser than atoms. The gravity of the universe acts upon the dark matter, shaping it into cosmic gobbets all connected by narrow filaments as the dark impulses of our collective consciousness shape our global society into collective clusters bound together by the fibril tissues of our social connectivity.

4.01] Observations of neutrinos are made deep within the Earth in places of profound darkness and quiet. So too must one seek these same conditions to make observations about the mysterious dark matter of our social structures, our institutions, and our unconscious. This distancing, displacement, solitude, and darkness are necessary for any meaningful understanding of social relations, which on the Earth's surface in the light of day and amidst the perpetual susurrus of our undertakings remain entirely unknowable. The psychic space comprised by the knowledge of the imminence of one's own death is one such place of refuge where one may come to understanding.

4.02] The absence of overpowering light is necessary to better understand light's subtle properties. This is why solar eclipses allow us to see what we normally cannot; observation of the 1919 total solar eclipse off the coast of west Africa allowed for the verification of the general theory of relativity Einstein published five years before.

4.03] In the same way solar eclipses allow us to understand cosmic phenomena, so too can instances of societal darkness provide a clear glimpse of the human. Arendt writes that totalitarian moments allow us to see the 'limits of our time' in a way we could not see them before. Totalitarianism is for Arendt the surfacing of the subterranean stream.

4.04] In understanding relations between one's self and others, one must not remain on the surface of things but go underground, boring down deep to where one may be cooled when one is overheated and warmed when one grows frigid in what has been deemed *psychothermal engineering*.

4.05] There are troubling parallels between the resource-extraction practice of hydraulic fracturing and the extraction of socio-economic resources from the populace through what has been deemed *psychic fracturing*. Proponents of *psychic fracturing* at first contended the methodology was more sustainable than previous techniques of extracting value from our social structures. But the externalized costs of this new approach quickly become apparent to any who care to see them, for they are as pernicious sociologically as the inadvertent effects of hydraulic fracturing are environmentally, effects which may include but are not limited to the presence of radionuclides in wastewater, the despoiling of aquifers, and the potential for greater earthquake activity.

5.00] One tries to consider social problems and their solutions with objectivity but cannot. Always the particular intrudes, contaminates. One cannot divorce these larger social quandaries from the particulars of one's own life, which so determine one's perspective. This is the problem of uncertainty, a distinctly human problem.

5.01] As one ages, one becomes increasingly liberated from the tyranny of self-regard while at the same time one becomes ever more entrenched in the particularities of the life one has lived, for there are more of these particularities with every passing day.

6.00] If all Life equals bacteria plus time $(L=b+t)$, it follows that one may deduce the sum total of time by subtracting the totality of all bacteria from Life $(t=L-b)$. We come to this deduction *in medias res*, for in our attempts to optimize our environment, to exert control over all facets of Life, we are systematically eradicating all bacteria. This will inevitably bring us face-to-face with the naked and unadulterated facticity of time, which we will never be able to bear, and which will inevitably overwhelm us just as the unmediated light of the sun blinds all those who look directly upon it.

6.01] If one contends, as did Wittgenstein, that eternity is the absence of time rather than time going on forever, then those who live in the here and now are immortal. Eternal Life equals bacteria.

6.02] One grows closer to death not because one's body is failing but because one exists increasingly in one's memories, which are neither here nor there. Memory is not an escape from time but the deadly trap of time. Memory is time's arrow through the heart.

7.00] In the backyard of one's childhood home one builds a castle in the sandbox with one's mother while one's brother kicks a ball and chases it, kicks it again. One recalls one's mother completely absorbed in play, utterly present with the shovel, the bucket, the sand, and the water that fleetingly gives it form.

7.01] This body, which one inhabits and which has served one for seven decades, allowing one to be in the world, to interface intellectually, emotionally, physically with others, is betraying one. It is turned inward against itself, mutating in ways that render it unsustainable. The pain of this betrayal is bound up with the physical pain. There is still a sense of disbelief, though the disbelief does not mitigate the pain. The pain does not care if one believes in it or not; it simply is. Sometimes it comes in the guise of an ache. It is a massive ghost that fills every room, every space one occupies. It is a generalized experience of inescapable suffering that wears one down. At other times it is like an invisible sword piercing one with a sharpness and specificity that seem exquisitely calculated, though the methodology remains opaque. The pain says, 'Feel me!' and one obeys. The pain says, 'Focus on me at the exclusion of all else!' and one is powerless to do anything but submit. One takes the medication provided. One waits for it to pass. Then one is left so spent and disoriented one does not know what to do in the absence of the pain, for the pain's intensity is such that in a short span of time it becomes so central to one's worldview that one is bereft, adrift, when left on one's own without one's pain as a companion.

7.02] From the perspective of eternity, *sub specie aeternitatis*, all one's suffering, frustrations, sadness are meaningless, infinitesimal, yet it is only from the perspective of suffering that one may perceive eternity. When one's suffering is finally at an end, so too, for one, does eternity – with its perspective on one's suffering – end.

8.00] Reason, when not grounded in something beyond reason, not grounded in some thing that cannot be arrived at through reason or articulated through language, becomes a force against itself, self-consuming, an Ouroboros. Suffering is not the only grounding but perhaps the one most firmly under one's feet, the ground that is most fecund and free of contaminants.

9.00] One recalls one's mother explaining Kuhn's account of the playing card experiment when one was still a child. One remembers her tone, the sense she was conveying something of importance. One remembers pride in being entrusted with this knowledge. The researchers, one's mother explained, presented volunteers with a series of playing cards the volunteers were asked to name. Among the regular cards were interspersed irregular cards such as a black four of hearts and a red six of spades. In almost every instance, the irregular cards were misidentified as normal cards. In most cases, the volunteers did not pause or notice anything at all out of the ordinary.

9.01] As a child, one was fascinated by this. How could the test subjects not notice what was directly in front of them? They knew they were participating in an experiment. This should have prepared them, one would think, to expect the unexpected.

9.02] What does it mean? one asked one's mother. Expectations shape the experience of reality, one's mother explained. Once one starts learning about the world, the colour of clubs (black) and spades (black) in a deck of playing cards, one comes to expect reality to conform to this understanding. It becomes extremely difficult to see things as they actually are, independent of one's expectation.

9.03] One remembers considering this for days afterward, while sitting at the dining room table with one's mother and brother, in moments of silence. One would think about this at night, when one would put down one's book, turn out the bedside light, and wait for sleep to come.

9.04] A week later, one found one's self alone with one's mother once again. It seemed necessary somehow to discuss the matter with her in private. If expectations shape reality, then what should be expected, in order to live the right way, one asks. Mother smiles. It is simple, she says. One should expect exactly the reality one wishes to live in. Let me give an example, she says. Imagine things are not as they should be, that there is inequity, corruption, greed, fear. In order to enable the possibility of change, one must expect that the change will come and that these wrongs will no longer exist in the way they do. In fact, one must prepare for this change to come by planning a great celebration for the occasion of the change. One must create an extravagant menu, including all the best things to eat, beautiful and delicious pastries and cakes. One must procure lavish and cheerful decorations, compose joyful music, rehearse it daily, hum its melodies while one goes about the preparations steadily, in anticipation of the imminent celebration.

9.05] This way of thinking, of living, one's mother explained, is sometimes dismissed as naivete, when in fact it is its opposite. So much enjoyment of anything lies in the anticipation, the looking forward. The enjoyment derived from anticipation is often greater than the enjoyment derived from the experience of the thing itself. When this sense of anticipation is combined with the very real preparations, one configures one's perception of reality so that the moment one hopes for may come to pass. The anticipation provides a sense of energy, of propulsion. This is not magical thinking or misplaced optimism. This is the power of purposeful action performed in good faith, not out of self-interest alone but self-interest subsumed into the interest of all those who may come to live their lives in the imminence of the celebration.

9.06] One at first accepts this on faith. One endeavours to live one's childhood in the state of anticipation of things improving.

9.07] A year passes. One's mother suffers a personal disappointment. One does not understand the cause but is keenly attuned to the change in her mood, her emotional distance. One evening one reminds her what she told one the year before. The reality, one's mother explains, is that the historical and social conditions around the desired occasion for the celebration are so complicated and immense that it is beyond any single individual, or indeed any limited group of individuals, to bring about the occasion. It is in effect beyond one's control. But the decision to expect it and to act toward it is not. Even if it does not occur in one's lifetime, one will derive purposefulness in the expectation of it and in acting on that expectation.

9.08] The beauty of childhood perception is that one may fully inhabit the fantastical reality of the story on its own terms while still intuiting the analogy. If the story has the imaginative power to sustain itself in the child's mind as the child ages, gradually the fantasy recedes, though the power of its memory lingers. Like a camera lens slowly shifting its focal point from the foreground to the background, the analogy comes into sharper relief with the passage of years as the fantasy becomes indistinct.

9.09] One becomes critical of this vision as one asserts one's independence. There are times in one's early adulthood when one rejects, on principle, all that one's mother attempted to impart. One may come back to one's mother's views from time to time when one feels lost, in what one would uncharitably describe as moments of weakness. One will adopt new ways of reckoning with them, rationalizing them, dismissing them. One will come to see this parable of the celebration as hypocritically spiritual, evangelical, as living in the world as one wishes it was rather than living in the world as it is. One comes to see the spurious promise of the celebration as a distraction from the truth of ongoing harm and the imperative to directly address this unnecessary suffering.

9.10] Then one comes around again. One considers, for instance, how focusing one's attention and energies on the imminent celebration and the necessity of its preparations may in fact deprive the oppressive regime of the primacy it holds in one's awareness, and as the hold on the power of the imaginary dissipates, so too does the hold on power in reality.

9.11] But what form, in this analogy, in the adult world, should the preparations for the celebration take? One may imagine them any way one pleases, and so one carries on as one sees fit.

9.12] Now one's death is imminent, and one is still preparing for the celebration, though one no longer believes that the celebration will occur in one's lifetime or in the lifetimes that come after. One still anticipates the tastes of the cakes and hums the melodies that one used to imagine would one day resound in every public square.

9.13] One realizes, as one tires of card games in the imminence of one's death, that everyone has been playing with a red six of spades. Everyone has been playing with this anomalous card, drawing it from the deck, holding it in their hand for a very long time, for forever, since the invention of playing cards. So far no one has noticed.

9.14] The more perceptive players have felt something, an indeterminate sense of unease when they have been dealt the red six of spades. These players have experienced a fleeting rush of nausea as their gaze swept over the card. They've suffered discomfort, vertigo, a sense of dislocation without ever knowing why. This has led them in their gameplay to hastily discard the red six of spades so that they no longer have to be in the presence of the card. They have done this without even being conscious of what they're doing.

9.15] Even the most perceptive players have not been able to see the red six of spades for what it is, their expectations being so configured by the deeply entrenched expectations of the four suits with the two colours: red and black, any deviation from this norm being literally unthinkable, though it is perhaps not imperceptible.

9.16] The irony is that what successes one has had in life are a result of understanding the four suits and their two colours as they have conventionally been understood, acting quickly, decisively, without hesitation or doubt in order to make the most, hand after hand after hand, of what one has been dealt, never questioning the dealer's motivations, never noticing that the House's take is always greater than that of all the players combined, let alone that the deck of cards does not conform to one's expectations of suit and rank.

9.17] What successes one has had in life are attributed to an unwillingness to compromise, a devotion to a cause, a cause that has some social worth, even if that worth has no immediate utility, even if it is only recognized by a few, even at great expense.

9.18] The way one has chosen to live that has resulted in one's successes is also the correct approach in times of crisis. Isn't the imminence of one's death the greatest crisis of all? The irony is that when death is imminent, one must abandon this way of thinking, this all-or-nothing approach, and instead embrace the incremental, the partial, the compromise, the imperfect, the pragmatic.

10.00] Benatar advocates for what he calls pragmatic pessimism. One may acknowledge the suffering that existence entails without succumbing to despair. One may derive meaning from useful pursuits without denying the harm that must always accompany existence. One may be clear-eyed about suffering, about the horrors of being, and not dwell on them, not be consumed by them, not deny them, but neither turn away from them toward an unguarded optimism.

10.01] Though within his book's very pages Benatar laments the unnecessary suffering caused by his own birth, in all sincerity and with great affection he dedicates the book to his parents.

10.02] It is the early morning hours of New Year's Day some forty years ago and one sits in one's brother's living room holding a glass of brandy. When one's mother has left the room, when one's sister-in-law and nieces have gone to bed, one's older brother, whose daughters are three and four years of age, tells one not to have children of one's own. It is hard for me, he says, but it would be all the worse for you because you are a woman, he says, not just any woman but the woman you are, with your ambition. Of course, one cannot know for certain, but one intuits that one's brother, despite his flaws, his distance, in spite of this statement, loves his children deeply. He tells one this not because he resents his own children, but because he thinks he knows his own sister and what's best for her, and what's best for her, given her disposition, the life he thinks she should lead, does not involve taking on the responsibilities of motherhood. It is not because of one's brother's advice but in spite of it that one goes through life childless. At some point one stopped caring about others' judgments about this, assumptions. But for years one first had to reckon with them. Most of the time they were unspoken. They could be inferred in the absence of speech, in a friend's unsuccessful attempt to suppress a facial expression. One always strove to meet this judgment with detachment. This judgment is about the person expressing it, one would tell one's self. From the position of the judger, one is the subject of this judgment about being childless, but this is not the correct position from which to view this relation, for the self that is being judged is not a self that submits to the terms of judgment. In fact, one categorically rejects the very framework in which the judgment is passed. One understands one's self as external to these mores, obligations, biological drives, instincts, even if that is not the way in which others see one. One's mother never brought it up. There was no overt pressure, thanks in part perhaps to one's brother's willingness to have children of his own, perhaps also in part thanks to the kind of difficult child one's brother once was. One's mother knew better. Often the assumption is that if one does not have children of one's own, one does not like them, or one fears them. Though there is no truth to this and in fact the opposite is true, this is an assumption it has been at times expeditious not to correct. One's nieces have always been a source of tremendous joy for one, a source of joy that motivated others to project upon one a desire to have children of one's own, as if the affection and love one feels for children at a remove must always be desired more closely and intimately, must be as direct and unmediated as possible, as if this is the only or the best or truest or most natural way to feel affection. On the contrary, some distance, some remove, can be a powerful mediator. The decision to become a parent or not become a parent, like so many decisions one makes in the course of living one's life, cannot be arrived at entirely through rational processes and must be made on a kind of leap of faith. So many underestimate the distance to the far side of the precipice as they launch themselves into the air. So many fall short, never reaching their intended goal, for the goal is misplaced in their mind, and once they lose contact with the solid ground, once they are airborne, there is no way for them to correct their course, nothing for them to push against. They remain helpless as their momentum dissipates and gravity takes hold.

10.03] One considers one's brother's advisement not to have children as one recalls being read to by one's mother. One was a child of four years old lying in bed while one's brother lay above in the top bunk reading his own book. One wonders to what extent he was aware of what one's mother was reading to one, a book she had surely read to him a few years before. How did the text read aloud by one's mother, the sound of those words in that room, interact with the words he was reading silently in the book of his own choosing? What was the amalgam of the textual and the oral, the relation between brother, sister, mother, text, reader, listener: one family unit, two children, one parent, two readers, two texts, three listeners, one bed, two bunks, three consciousnesses in relation to one another and in relation to the ebbing day. One's brother, one imagines, decades later, putting one's self in his perspective many nights ago, is simultaneously annoyed at the intrusion of his mother's reading while he is trying to read and reassured by the sound of her voice as she reads to his younger sister, this reassuring imposition on his nascent sense of autonomy, this soft presence of the two of them, mother, sister, on the bed beneath him, communing with one another through the mediation of the pages of the storybook that was once his and that he would one day go on to read to his own children. One thinks, for one's self, the contentment, warmth, restfulness and security of that moment is perhaps as far removed as possible from the experience of suffering, an interstice in a continuum of living consciousness in which pain is fundamental, primary, unavoidable.

11.00] Thirty years ago, when one's mother was about the age one is now, one goes to visit her. It is March. The sky is overcast. One sits with her at the dining room table, drinking tea. Though it is early afternoon, one's mother still wears her dressing gown. There is a period of silence. These are not uncommon for one's mother, particularly as she has aged, though this instance has a unique intensity. It is as if, one thinks, she is contemplating her own mortality. She is not ill, as one will be when one is the age one's mother is now. But perhaps she realizes that her life will not last much longer. Then suddenly, confirming one's suspicions, she tries to articulate something of what life has been like for her. She says that her life has seemed like a visit to an art gallery. The gallery, she says, has been hosting a retrospective by a renowned painter. It is the last week of the exhibition. The walls are adorned by large, lavish canvases demanding close attention. Her life, she says, has been like being dragged through this gallery by a petulant child. She has wished to engage with the works around her. But the child, with interests of his own, has not allowed it. The child has no interest in the paintings, seeing the gallery as a kind of trial to be endured as hastily as possible. There is nothing for the child to do in the gallery, and its quietude disturbs him. One's mother pauses then, looking one in the eye, as if to gauge the effect her words have had. She urges one not to misinterpret what she has said. It is only an analogy. She realizes it is a distasteful one. The child in her analogy, one's mother says, is purely figurative. It is not meant to reflect her actual daughter or her son, whom she has always loved. Speaking of this figurative child is merely the best way for her to express her experience of life. It has nothing to do with her having actually been a mother, not directly. Let her explain, she says. She has a duty to safeguard this figurative child, to remain with him. She cannot coerce him into lingering in the gallery against his will. If she attempts to do so, the child will protest, causing a disruption that would disturb the dignity of the gallery for the other patrons. As he tugs on her hand and pulls her through the gallery, she sees him glance at a painting, turn away. She attempts to engage him in conversation about colour, form. What do you see? she asks, as his attention wanes. He looks at another painting, pausing. This one features a mischievous boy his own age, black-haired, green-eyed. It's caught his attention. Who's that, she asks him. What do you think his name is? The child loses interest and pulls her onward. She implores the child to take his time, to be patient. Let's make a game of it, decide which ones are our favourites, she suggests, to no avail. She attempts to bribe him with the promise of an ice cream, if only he will give her a moment to look. Every attempt to engage the child, to slow him down, only increases his petulance. As much as she resents his impatience, she admires his wilfulness. They are just paintings, she tells herself. What really matters is her presence in the child's life, the child's presence in her life in this moment. Perhaps, she thinks, the importance of the paintings is to create an event, an occasion for her to spend time with her son. She asks herself to what extent she is really interested in the paintings. Is it the paintings themselves that interest her, or the idea of them, the mystique of the painter, the mystery of the artist at work? Do they speak to her? Would they possess the capacity to move her if she were granted an adequate opportunity to engage with them? Are they really that much more impressive in person? Or is her interest aspirational? Maybe the petulant child, she thinks, with his complete lack of pretension, of aspiration, is expressing her true attitude to the paintings in hurrying past them. It is possible, she thinks, that these paintings provided some usefulness at the time they were created, but that they no longer need to be displayed and observed and contemplated. They have served their purpose, made their contribution but no longer need to take up all this space and attention. Perhaps she can be glad they existed, can benefit in some indirect way from living in a world in which they came to be without ever having seen them properly or even thought about them. She's been told before that art has value precisely because it has no utility. But she's never thought this to be true. It is, if anything, a gross oversimplification. Art does have utility. But that utility is so complex and diffuse as to be virtually impossible to quantify and so it needs to be taken on a kind of faith. She does not really believe what she tried to convince herself about the paintings no longer mattering. This was only a failed attempt to rationalize away her frustration at not being able to see them properly because of the child. She could still love the petulant child while being frustrated by him. She would come back later, without the child. The paintings were important enough to her that she experience them while unencumbered. But no, she knew. Despite her best intentions, this would never happen. It was the final week of the exhibition and her life was very busy. It is with great disappointment that she acquiesces to the petulant child, leaving the gallery, which in this analogy is equivalent to death. At least, she said, she got a passing glimpse of the paintings, got to be in their presence for a few minutes. That's more than most people get. Then she stops speaking. She looks out the window, as if to give one time to understand what she has said. One sits there, considers the strange and disquieting description. One asks one's mother: what are the paintings in this analogy? What are they supposed to represent? Everything, she says. Living. Hopes, dreams, intentions. But what is their subject matter? one asks. What are the paintings of? Her life, says one's mother. Childhood, adolescence, adulthood. Mundane afternoons. Forgotten moments. A few milestones. Pictures of her parents, friends, lovers, her children, colleagues, neighbours. There were some beautiful ones of you, of your brother, she said, that she didn't get more than a glance of. She does not appear in any of the paintings, but she is present in all of them. What about the child, one asks. He's not real, she says. He exists only for the purposes of the analogy. But what does he represent, one asks. Obligation, she says, circumstance, the inevitable, responsibility to self and others, aging, physical and mental decline, the relentless passage of time. Will the child remember anything of the gallery, one asks. Of course not, she says. But then, after a pause, she says that the child in the analogy would go on to live his life, having no memory whatsoever of that gallery visit imposed on him or how he managed to circumvent its monstrous tedium through sheer determination. Perhaps, she said, the visit to the gallery will have instilled on the fictional child in her analogy some unconscious impression, which – if it was not outweighed by resentment – would open up new possibilities for him at a later point in his life, figuratively speaking.

11.01] Heisenberg writes that though analogies have their limitations they nevertheless allow one to express things that language otherwise cannot as one lacks the terms. Language, writes Heisenberg, was created for the purposes of daily life and fails one at the level of the atom, for language emerged in order to describe experiences involving vast quantities of atoms grouped together.

11.02] Arendt writes that Wittgenstein's aphorism 'what we cannot speak of must remain unspoken' applies to the objects we sense and not just to experience of the senses.

11.03] When one's mother died in her sleep some months later, one remembered her analogy and then tried to forget it. One has never shared it with anyone, not even one's brother.

12.00] When death is imminent and one knows it and one insists on trying to expand or deepen one's understanding, one is not truly reckoning with the concepts one encounters themselves but simply encountering death. The specific text does not matter. It is all death, death, death in syntactical variation and subtly differing typefaces.

13.00] One spends a lifetime calibrating the correct ratio of pleasure, indulgence, rest to stress, exertion, pain: a highly individual equation. If one is privileged and wise, if material and social conditions permit, as one ages one achieves some mastery in the application of this formula. Then in the imminence of one's death the ratio needs to be recalibrated entirely.

14.00] One positions one's self upon the chesterfield in one's study, the chesterfield that historically provided a place for reading in the afternoons, when the desk grew wearisome, doubling on rare occasions as a place for overnight guests to sleep. In the early stages of one's illness one would shuttle each day between this chesterfield and one's bed. As one's condition worsened, it has become more or less one's permanent post. One has thus assumed the status of guest in one's own home.

14.01] Fixtures of this room that one overlooked for years now become intimate companions. The print of Dürer's *Young Hare* inherited from one's maternal grandmother, brought by steamship across the Atlantic. Its presence in this room, hastily hung there some four decades before out of a necessity of putting something on the study wall, is some concession to lineage, continuity. One has a fondness for it though it is not aesthetically pleasing. It gives one something to stare at: the tufts of tousled fur, the latent menace of its claws.

14.02] The off-white paint on the walls of the study which was perfectly adequate for decades now seems sloppy, inexpertly applied. How could one spend so much time in this room and never notice this before? Of course, there were always so many other details with which to occupy one's attention. The meeting of the two shades of off-white at ceiling and wall is haphazard, as if the border where one begins and the other ends could not be readily discerned, as if the painter couldn't decide where to draw the line, even though the division of wall and ceiling is so unequivocally articulated by the ninety-degree angle at which the two meet. If one were to live only a few months longer than one suspects one will live, one would insist on repainting, no matter the impracticality, no matter the inconvenience. If nothing else, one's stubborn and irrational insistence on repainting one's death chamber would provide the housepainters a story to share with their intimates after a day's work.

14.03] The study has the virtue of a window upon the yard with a view of one's garden. The last few summers one has stopped tending it. It is going back to nature. In this way, in the gradual effacement of the physical assertions of one's will, this rewilding patch of land is a harbinger of one's imminent absence. How quickly the space one once occupied is reclaimed, overtaken, overgrown. One does not begrudge nature for reclaiming dominion over itself. In fact, one wishes a great forest to arise where the garden once was, gargantuan trees to tower above where the radishes once grew.

14.04] There is only the silver birch in the far corner of the yard. Somehow on its spindly branches a few leaves have persisted through the winter. They must soon give way, one thinks, or else perhaps they may inhibit the growth of the spring buds, the opening of which one will likely not live to see.

15.00] The memories that persist and come to one unbidden seem completely arbitrary. They are not the things one wishes to remember or memories that one feels to be particularly important. Instead they impose themselves upon one's consciousness in the same way that the seeming randomness of reality imposes itself on the course of one's life.

15.01] Certain early memories become foundational. They take on a significance in one's life that often transcends any objective understanding of the import of the events on which they are based. For whatever reason they become, in time, central to one's self-understanding.

15.02] At times one's condition is such that one no longer has the capacity for thought while at the same time one feels a pressing urgency to articulate the content of one's mind in language, if for no one but one's self.

15.03] In dying, too, one must balance one's self-interest with the larger concerns of one's community, of others, though the weight of each has shifted with circumstance. What more can others expect of one who is dying? What more do the others require of one? What more does one who is dying want others to want? What more does one have to give?

15.04] If others require nothing more of one, then for the others death is deprived of some of its power, for death does not then have the power to deprive.

15.05] If others still require something of one, then this creates pressure, a stress, a force of resistance for one to push against, a reason to live even as life slips away.

15.06] One grows so accustomed to being alone that one can't imagine living the end of one's life in any other circumstance. One can imagine it, perhaps, but one does not desire it. Arendt writes that the difference between solitude and loneliness is that loneliness only ever arises when one is alone and fails to divide one into two. So long as one remains capable of thinking, one can never be alone for one is necessarily conscious of one's self. The thinking self is divided not against one's self but rather against loneliness, divided in favour of the company the thinking self provides one when no other but the self is present.

16.00] In the beginning one lived fully and freely, with the grace and exuberance of naïveté. Only with the passage of years did the self-consciousness begin to take hold, the fear of failure, of judgment. The result was the hardening of sensibility, the rigid perfectionism, the calculated tone, which was not without a frigid beauty, a beauty for which one was lauded, praised, a beauty that adhered to itself like a plaque building up in the arteries. Only the imminence of death flushes it out so the blood can flow freely once again.

16.01] Kuhn writes that the ones who make the breakthroughs are young, in the early years of their maturity, versed in the discipline but not yet fully indoctrinated into its orthodoxies. Their thinking is supple. There is the line from the Russian film: 'Death is old, hard, strong. Youth is supple, weak, pliable.' Can one relinquish hardness and strength? Can one abandon force of will through force of will? One can become supple, weak, pliable in the imminence of one's death when one's strength abates. One discovers there can be suppleness and pliability in the fear and humility that come with the imminence of non-existence.

16.02] One has to let go of what one holds dear before one can grasp something new. One is wary of relinquishing one's grasp, for it sustains one, though it does so at great cost to one's self and to others. There is immense vulnerability in the letting go, the surrendering, a necessary faith that what one gives up will be replaced by something that better serves one. The letting go will be terrifying. One must give up a certain fate for one that is uncertain, and even though that which is certain is disastrous, at least it is knowable and that makes it less terrifying than it should be, less terrifying than it is.

16.03] One has now begun the process of loosening one's grasp, for one way or another, willingly or unwillingly, what one grasps will inevitably be taken. Which is more dignified: to clutch at it with desperation until the end or to relinquish with resignation?

16.04] Sometimes one finds it liberating to view one's personal affairs from the cosmic perspective. How paltry, petty, they seem from this vantage. At other times one finds it horribly oppressive, all those heavenly bodies hurtling through an ever-expanding vastness. The burgeoning mass of the cosmos presses down upon one if one thinks about it for too long, rendering one incapable even of changing one's soiled clothing.

16.05] Wittgenstein wished he had written a work of philosophy consisting entirely of jokes. The only reason he didn't, he said, is that he had no sense of humour.

16.06] When the home care nurse comes to take one's readings, to sample, prod, one catches her looking around at one's environs, taking in the books and dust. She does not know it is not that much worse than it was before one became ill. One has battled with dust all one's life. Sometimes the dust gathers around hair and assumes larger forms. They are more formidable than mere bunnies. They are dust hares, with all the presence of Dürer's watercolour.

16.07] It is the nurse who will find one's remains one day, as she has no doubt come upon the remains of others.

16.08] One day in the hallway between the bedroom and the bathroom, one's left knee gives way. There is reassurance in the resounding thud as one hits the ground, that an old woman falling down with no one to hear her is still substantial enough to make a sound!

16.09] One lies prone on the hardwood floor, considering one's state of affairs. One spies a dust hare on the floor, at eye level. One examines it with keen interest, the way in which the hair and the particles of dust and detritus are attracted to and bond with one another. It has a surprising heft in the palm. If one cannot beat the dust, one should join the dust.

16.10] Each time one wakes one wonders if one will still be able to function as well as one did the day before, if the same faculties will still be at one's disposal: mobility, cognition, executive function. Pain accompanies all of these to various degrees, transforming what were once everyday tasks into momentous accomplishments. One refuses to suffer pain gladly.

17.00] For one who lives a life preoccupied with form, with narratives, understanding, causation, context, relation, there is a strange satisfaction in knowing one's own approximate terminus, even if it is not one that one would have chosen, even if the home stretch is rather more uncomfortable than many of the stretches that came before, the scenery rather more mundane. Knowing the approximate terminus allows one to see the form of one's life, the shape of it from start to finish, so that one may make observations about the ebb and flow between the two.

This is another unexpected but not insignificant luxury, to spend one's final weeks considering what has played out over the decades. The consideration is suffused with physical pain and decline. The consideration perhaps mitigates the suffering, though the suffering still flavours the consideration.

17.01] One remains suspicious to the end that there is any narrative at all, at least one with meaning, one about which one can draw conclusions. Narratives are reassuring, entertaining. The problem is that the meaning always originates from the ambiguity of the narrative. The narrative is always a reduction of reality, even a reduction of a fantasy about reality in the fantasizer's mind. The narrative is always a simplification in language, image, sound, of something so complex as to be irreducible. Always one strives to reduce being to a scale so that it is understandable, digestible, containable, communicable. As soon as one acquires self-understanding, knowledge, one starts narrativizing. All the meanings linked to one's values, decision-making, are linked to narratives. Nothing exists in and of itself but only in relation to its context. The attempt to narrativize always does injustice to both the representation of the context and also to the existent, the it. One is compelled with tremendous urgency to understand the narratives, to incorporate others' narratives into one's personal narrative, always editing, revising, realigning the symbolic order so it is true to who one is at that given moment, true to the complexity of understanding of which one is capable in that instant, accurately corresponding to the emotional thrust (tragic, comic, ambivalent, catastrophic) of that time. One day the narrative might free one from itself, if one just gets it right. One day one might be able to be as one is without the balm of narrative. In the purity of suffering without narrative's intercession, one will realize one's potential for freer and truer modes of understanding. One's reality will be complete in and of itself in a way that one can understand without beginning or end, without the need for exegesis. One is not there yet, but one meditates on this as one considers how the imminence of one's death reconfigures all the events that led up to it. The lead-up to death makes an intelligible narrative out of one's life. Among the many impositions one is freed of at the moment of death is the drive to understanding through narrative. Until then one must work within the medium of memory.

17.02] John of Patmos writes in the Book of Revelation, 'And when the seven thunders had uttered their voices, I was about to write: and I heard a voice from heaven saying unto me, Seal up those things which the seven thunders uttered and write them not.' Whenever one feels the urge to make sense of being one should first consider these words.

17.03] Or, perhaps one should instead honour the divine wisdom of the seven thunders and hold their utterances in one's memory only. There one's remembering can fade, distort, embellish, bend to one's purposes. One may hear the seven thunders in one's mind until they eventually go silent.

17.04] Before one advanced in years takes on a new memory, one should consider for a moment that one's bank of memories may be fixed in its capacity. Once one's memory is full, it cannot retain new memories unless the old ones are overwritten. One will not have control over which memories are erased. It will not necessarily be the oldest ones, for the system of memory organization, management, and updating continues to defy one's understanding, indeed, grows ever further from the capacity of one's understanding as time passes. One must simply accept that after a certain point, one takes on new memories at the peril of the old ones.

17.05] One thinks of one's friends, most of whom have already ceased to exist. One feels no urgency in trying to see for a last time those who still live and suffer. This is a wish of one for whom death is not imminent but who tries and fails to imagine what the reality of imminent death might be like. Instead, as one goes about one's final days, one remembers fleetingly, in passing, an inside joke, a gesture of kindness, and is surprised to find that this sometimes adequately mitigates the relentlessness of one's suffering.

17.06] One thinks of one's family, most of whom have already ceased to exist. One thinks of one's nieces. One reflects on the fact that it is possible to have a difficult relationship with one's brother in adulthood but to have a deep affection for his children. This is one of the eventualities of life that is impossible to predict or understand. One derives an irrational comfort from the thought that one's nieces may go on living their lives for decades after one has died. One will have no knowledge of this, whether they are pleased with their own state of affairs, whether they make peace with their own allotments of suffering, with the decisions that they make and the circumstances that existence visits upon them. One imagines them thinking of one after one has died, recalling their aunt who always took what seemed to be a disproportionate interest in their lives. One imagines them remembering her and laughing, taking delight at their recollection of her unseemliness. In this way one does not live on exactly but some remnant of one's existence takes on new forms that are inextricably entwined with the existence of the rememberers.

17.07] The observer effect applies to memory. One cannot remember anything without necessarily altering the memory. This is not a limitation of the memory itself but a quality of the relationship between subject and object, viewer and viewed, one and an other, rememberer and memory.

17.08] Every time one recalls a memory, holds it before the mind's eye, one distorts it. It becomes tarnished with emotions and desires, encrusted with all the remnants of other memories, experiences, with interpretation, the psychic detritus of life. In this way, each time one accesses the memory, the memory becomes further distanced from the specificity of the moment in time from which it is derived.

17.09] The memory one possesses that is the purest is the memory one has forgotten.

17.10] This memory surfaces only after many decades of languishing in the recesses of one's cerebral cortex. It is summoned by the texture of a hair, the smell of dust.

17.11] One must be conservative in one's remembering. One must make an effort not to recall one's most cherished memories too frequently for fear of distorting them. One must safeguard one's essence by developing techniques of distancing, depersonalization, generalization, a guardedness in one's language, in one's thinking, in one's relation to one's own experience.

17.12] A luxury emerging in the imminence of one's death is that one can indulge one's memories. There is no longer any reason to preserve them through forgetting, for they will be permanently forgotten soon enough. One may even with a clean conscience profane the perfection of one's most cherished memory by committing it to paper.

17.13] I am nine years old and it is summer. I am walking through a meadow in the countryside. It is late in the afternoon on a Sunday at the end of August. The light is resplendent and golden. I feel the grasses on the bare skin of my legs. I am walking toward home, my mother following behind me. My brother is not with us. Though I miss him, I am delighted to have my mother to myself this day. This is the longest my brother has ever been away. My missing him does not detract from the contentment I feel in this moment because I know he is happy where he is. I know that he misses our mother, misses me, and that he will be with us again soon. His absence is like the summer break from school, to which I looked forward and enjoy, though I miss my friends, my teacher. Summer is drawing to a close. Even at this age I have some understanding that life will not go on forever. I look back at my mother. Her stride is unhurried. She looks toward the forest at the edge of the meadow. When I was very young, I used to delight in playing in this forest, in running into it as quickly as I could. I wished to lose myself in it instantly, eluding my family, entering into another, secret realm. At the age of five, a great fear of the forest suddenly arose in me. I could no longer enter into it, not even along a path, not even while clutching my mother's hand. At the age of five the fear of the forest was the same as my fear that my mother would die and I would have to be in the world without her. At the age of five my experience of suffering was limited but my imagination was at its peak. By the age of nine, the fear of the forest has subsided into a wariness, which is overpowered by my curiosity. As I walk through the meadow I look toward the forest's edge. The presence of its depths enriches the beauty of the open meadow. Now, as I recall this memory for the last time, immersing myself in it fully, a shift occurs in my perspective. I no longer see the meadow, the forest, my mother, through the eyes of nine-year-old me. I am present in that space and moment, but I am also outside of time. I am no longer in that child's body. I see myself now from without, nine years old, walking through the meadow. I see this from just inside the forest's edge, looking out into the light which has deepened and intensified just before it starts to wane. I see my mother, the swaying grasses. I am struck by her youth, the quietude of her love. I see the world of late summer as it was more than six decades before. I feel it, inhabit it, as if that space and time were here and now, my gaze panoramic, drinking it in, as my vantage point recedes into that forest, gradually, the child, the mother, making their leisurely progress home, as the point from which I see them, from which I take them in, pulls steadily, inexorably, further into the forest, where already it is evening, the day having ended barely after it began, the shadows never relinquishing their hold on everything beneath the verdant canopy above.

'All meaning is created through crisis and diffusion.'

Acknowledgements

Jean Marc Ah-Sen: I would like to acknowledge the support of my family, friends, and fellow 'Disintegrationists.' I owe a special debt of gratitude to Katrina Lagacé, my little mudlarks, Samantha Haywood, Lynn Crosbie, Naben Ruthnum, André Forget, Paul Pope, Allison LaSorda, Dakota McFadzean, *Ro.Go.Pa.G.*, Ingrid Paulson, Alana Wilcox, James Lindsay, Crystal Sikma, and Coach House Books.

Emily Anglin: Thanks go to many more people than I can list here, but among them, special thanks go to Jean Marc Ah-Sen for inviting me to be a part of this book and for bringing it together. Thanks also go to Alana, James, and everyone at Coach House for all of their support of the project.

Devon Code: The author wishes to express his gratitude to Jean Marc Ah-Sen, Rob Sternberg, Jules Lewis, Dennis Vanderspek, Alana Wilcox, and Carolyn Code.

Lee Henderson: With gratitude and acknowledgements to historian Gwendolen Webster and her research into Kurt Schwitters and his internment, without which this piece could not have been written.

About the Authors

Jean Marc Ah-Sen is the author of *In the Beggarly Style of Imitation* and *Grand Menteur*, which was selected as one of the 100 best books of 2015 by the *Globe and Mail*. The *National Post* has hailed his work as 'an inventive escape from the conventional.' He lives in Toronto with his wife and two sons.

Writer and freelance editor **Emily Anglin** grew up in Waterloo, Ontario, and now lives in Toronto. She holds an MA in Creative Writing from Concordia University and a PhD in English from Queen's University. Emily Anglin's first collection of short fiction, *The Third Person*, was published in 2017 (Book*hug). She is currently at work on her first novel.

Devon Code is a fiction writer. He is the author of *Involuntary Bliss*, a novel, and *In A Mist*, a collection of stories. In 2010, he was the recipient of the Writers' Trust Journey Prize. Originally from Dartmouth, Nova Scotia, he lives in Peterborough, Ontario.

Lee Henderson is the author of three books, a collection of short stories and two novels, all published with Penguin. A contributing editor for *Border Crossings* magazine for over fifteen years and cover curator for *The Malahat Review* since 2015, he also teaches creative writing at the University of Victoria. His visual art has been exhibited in Canada and abroad.

Typeset in Arno and Linotype Didot.

Printed at the Coach House on bpNichol Lane in Toronto, Ontario, on Zephyr Antique Laid paper, which was manufactured, acid-free, in Saint-Jérôme, Quebec, from second-growth forests. This book was printed with vegetable-based ink on a 1973 Heidelberg KORD offset litho press. Its pages were folded on a Baumfolder, gathered by hand, bound on a Sulby Auto-Minabinda, and trimmed on a Polar single-knife cutter.

Coach House is on the traditional territory of many nations including the Mississaugas of the Credit, the Anishnabeg, the Chippewa, the Haudeno-saunee, and the Wendat peoples and is now home to many diverse First Nations, Inuit, and Métis peoples. We acknowledge that Toronto is covered by Treaty 13 with the Mississaugas of the Credit. We are grateful to live and work on this land.

Edited by Alana Wilcox
Cover design by Ingrid Paulson, photo ©iStockPhoto/Galina Chetvertina
Interior design by Crystal Sikma
Interior illustrations by Dakota McFadzean

Coach House Books
80 bpNichol Lane
Toronto, ON M5S 3J4
Canada

416 979 2217
800 367 6360

mail@chbooks.com
www.chbooks.com